What's
the Matter
with
Wakefield?

What's the Matter with Wakefield?

June Lewis Shore

Illustrated by David K. Stone

ABINGDON PRESS
Nashville and New York

Library of Congress Cataloging in Publication Data

SHORE, JUNE LEWIS, 1930-
  What's the matter with Wakefield?
  SUMMARY: "Borrowing" the class money to buy him-
self a special fishing rod brings Wakefield much grief when
he is unable to pay it back.
  [1. Family life—Fiction. 2. Christmas stories] I. Stone,
David K., illus.   II. Title.
PZ7.S55868Wh   [Fic]   73-16040

ISBN 0-687-44908-1

For

Stephen
Susan
Rebecca
Alison
Melissa

CHAPTER

1

The school was spooky quiet, like in the jungle movies when the music stops and the alligator slithers down the bank. Nobody slammed lockers, nobody edged books off the desk. The only person in all three floors of Highview Elementary was Wakefield Kennedy Quinn. (Well, George, the janitor, was there, but he was definitely not in a talking mood.) Usually Wakefield stacked up his books five minutes before the last bell, and he and Paul Harris raced each other for the front door. But today was different. Today he didn't want to go home.

He looked in people's desks for a while, unfolded notes and read them, and folded them into little squares again. He tried out Miss Booth's swivel chair until he got dizzy, and then checked under her blotter for slips from the office. Miss Booth would have liked all the silence, he thought—she liked silence almost better than neatness—but not him. He picked up her paperweight and rapped for attention. *Bang!* The sound clanged and echoed through the empty school like a dynamite blast. George, who was scraping snow scenes off the windows with a razor blade, looked up cross as a bear.

"Hey, George, how come the owners of the lost dog didn't put an ad in the newspaper for him?"

George mumbled something about hearing that joke only forty times this week, and it was because the dog couldn't read.

Everybody in the fourth grade thought it was a neat joke. Even Miss Booth had laughed. But George kept on sweeping up paper chains with the push broom, going around and around the room until all the beautiful decorations were heaped up into an ugly mound. Usually the two had good talks, but now George snapped, "Don't bother me, boy. I'm in a hurry. Want to start my Christmas vacation, same as you."

Wakefield knew he should go home; mothers get cranky when you don't report in after school. It wasn't that he wanted to stay at school that much, but he didn't want to start his vacation either. Last year, when he was eight, it had been different. He did the same goofy things his little sister was doing now. He wrote letters to Santa Claus and looked in the snow for reindeer tracks. But a boy of nine—almost ten—is a little bit old for make-believe elves and ho-ho-ho.

His mom and dad were having a great time this Christmas. They whispered secrets to each other—"Did you get the *you-know-what* for *you-know-who*"—and then made a big thing of locking the *you-know-what* in the *you-know-where,* which was the back hall closet. They were having a Few-Friends-In, too. Wakefield asked right off if he could come, but his parents decided he definitely wouldn't enjoy it, that a boy of nine was really too young for grown-up fun.

That was his chief problem: He was never the right age. He was too young for the Few-Friends-In; he was too old for Santa Claus.

"This is going to be a long, stupid Christmas," he told George. "How come we get out of school on the tenth?"

George mumbled something about the Board of Education's having to replace the boiler and it was about time, if you asked him. He'd already dumped the big metal cans, put away the broom, and was standing at the outside door. Without speaking, he locked up behind Wakefield and started for the snow-rimmed parking lot. Suddenly George turned happy. He yelled back, "Merry Christmas,

Wakefield. Don't work too hard," and almost ran to his car.

There was nothing to do but start Christmas.

When George's car had slushed out of sight, Tag-Along Toomey edged around the corner of the building. He was carrying a scruffy-looking basketball in one hand and holding up his jeans with the other.

"Hey Wake! Wanna shoot some baskets?"

That was Tag-Along—shooting baskets with a foot and a half of snow on the ground. He looked up at Wake with big pale blue eyes, like a puppy dog begging at the table. Wakefield wondered if what they said was true, that Tag cut his hair with the hedge clippers. There was a lots of it, at any rate, yellow-white, all jagged around the edges.

"Guess not, Tag."

"Let me walk home with you, okay? Halfway?"

What else could you say but sure? There was really nothing wrong with Tag. There was nothing exactly right about him either. He was one of these people Wakefield's mother insisted he be nice to—like church ladies and relatives who pinch your cheek hard and say, "My, how you have grown."

"Mad Dog wants to fight you, Wake," Tag said. "You gonna fight him back?" Mad Dog Hennessey was a sixth-grader, tall for his age, and tough. (He had four older brothers and a father who was very big on judo.) Other kids in the neighborhood collected matchbook covers or bottle caps, but Mad Dog's hobby was fighting. And he didn't have to be steamed up to start something; he just liked to fight.

"I'm not allowed. Dad says I have to understand Mad Dog, get close to him."

"Understand Mad Dog?" Tag's white eyebrows raised half an inch.

"Don't ask me how I'm supposed to understand a creep who smashes toad frogs and raids birds' nests."

"Yeah, Mad Dog's rotten. All bad." Tag always agreed with everything Wakefield said. If Wake had said the earth was square, Tag would've said, "Yeah, yeah, you bet."

"And getting close to Mad Dog Hennessey"—Wakefield slammed a snowball at a garbage can. "Well, you might as well snuggle up to a giant squid. Or wade into a school of piranhas."

"Parents!" Tag spat a nice arc which cut through the snow piled up against the sidewalk. Wake didn't know how Tag knew so much about parents. His mother had been dead a long time, and his father had a "problem." Having a problem, though people never came right out

11

and said it, meant being in jail a lot. *D and D*, the newspapers called it: *Drunk and disorderly conduct.*

"So what about Mad Dog, Wake?"

Wakefield didn't have a ready answer. He'd been given strict orders to stay out of trouble. "No more fighting," his dad said. "You must learn to solve your problems through discussion and compromise." So what was he supposed to do? Be known all over Highview as "Old Yellow Belly"?

"You want me to help you fight him, Wake?"

Wakefield looked down at Tag-Along. A fair-sized sneeze could blow him away. "Guess not, Tag. I'll work something out."

They kicked a rock all the way to Center Street. It skittered off into traffic then, which neither minded; rock-kicking is only good for a couple of blocks. Besides, they found themselves in front of Sutcliff's Sporting Goods. Tag was already darting from one window to the next, his breath making a row of misty circles on the glass.

Wakefield ambled over to Sutcliff's major display, took one look, and couldn't move another step. Arranged on folds of gold cloth was an eight-foot, three-and-a-half-ounce fiberglass fly rod, with six gold-plated guides and a gold-plated tip: the *Geronimo 300,* long and sleek and shiny black, its gold parts twinkling under the lights of Mr. Sutcliff's artificial tree. A single-action fly reel with its own canvas pouch lay beside it. Above it, resting on top of the empty boxes, were two spools of top quality fly line—Number 6 sinking and Number 7 floating. The writing on the box assured the serious sportsman that Geronimo lines were "superbly balanced to deliver the fly with delicacy." There were forward tapered monofilament leaders—"soft, supple, and strong"—and a divided plastic box containing four lures: a popper, a plastic worm, and two flies—the *Royal Coachman* and the *Yellow May*—which, according to the label on the case, were hand-tied in Kenya, Africa.

What a beauty! A person could go for the fighters with that outfit: the *speckles* and *rainbows* and *smallmouth bass*. He'd caught about a million blue gill at Lake Belle, and last fall he caught the limit on croppie; but he'd never, ever battled a really great fish to a standstill. But what could you expect with a cane pole? *A cane pole,* for goodness' sake!

Wakefield suddenly became aware of a shadowy blur that had been hanging over the *Geronimo 300* much too long. It was the reflection of the ickiest girl in Highview Elementary, Imogene Cooke. Imogene was the kind of a girl who always reminded the teacher to collect the

homework papers. She'd also ask when the book reports were due, and if she knew half the class didn't have theirs, she'd ask several times.

He and Tag turned to face Imogene, but nobody said "hello." Finally, Imogene drew her neck up long and announced that she was going to buy skates. "Ice skates, of course."

"Big deal," Wake said.

"I have my own money, you know." She took out her billfold and counted it. "Seven, eight, nine, ten. Oh,

here's a five I didn't know I had."

"Big deal," Tag said.

Wakefield turned back to the fly rod.

Very few people ignored Imogene Cooke! "You can't fool me, Wake," she sputtered. "I bet right now you wish you could have that old fishing thing you're looking at. But *you* haven't got the money, have you?"

"Oh, I guess I'd get it if I really wanted it."

"Ha— ha— ha," Imogene sang the words, stringing out each ha until she'd backed up to Sutcliff's entrance.

For a minute Wakefield held his breath; it looked as though Imogene might get her pony tail caught in the closing door. She didn't. The very last hair eased by just in the nick of time. Nothing bad ever happened to Imogene Cooke.

After one more long look at the Geronimo—*Man, what a beauty!*—he and Tag left. Neither one wanted to face Imogene when she came out with the ice skates.

"Guess they'd be solid gold," Wakefield said.

Tag agreed.

They walked on without talking, not even bothering to miss the cracks, until they got to the Burger Barn at First and Center. Just then the big double doors of the Barn opened, and the good rich smell of french fries swirled all around them.

"You got any money, Wake?" Both boys had stopped in the middle of the sidewalk.

Wakefield shook his head no. Then remembering, he snapped his fingers. "Have I got money! Look here, Tag." He unzipped his parka, unbuttoned the pocket of his shirt, and took out a handful of bills and loose change.

Tag was impressed. "I never seen that much money!"

"I never *saw* that much money," Wake corrected.

"You never seen that much money neither? Wow!"

Tag had that puppy dog look again
malt or something?"

"No, this money belongs to the cl
sale and dues and all, twenty-four do
cents. I have to buy an aquarium the
because the Pet Palace is having a s
closest."

"Miss Booth trusted you with all

"Sure she did." Wakefield smootl
folded them carefully in half. "Of co
talk with me first."

Tag nodded. He and Miss Booth
little talks. Miss Booth usually did

"You know what she wanted m
me to pin the money to my coat. In
my name and address on it."

"But you talked her out of it, did
was full of admiration. "Just think
if you lost it. I'd be so afraid." He r
heaven. Tag was afraid of many th
down the fire escape at school; he
garter snake; he thought the boog
him.

Wakefield smiled. "I don't plan
The doors of the Burger Barn

17

e high school girls came out munching hamburgers
carrying malts in paper cups. "You don't think we
d sort of . . . just *borrow* some money from the class,"
suggested. "Just enough for french fries? We could
."

Not really, Tag." The problem with Tag was that
d no control.

ey walked in opposite directions then, throwing
balls at each other until they got out of range. Tag
at the bottom end of Center where the railroad
the paint factory and the lumberyards were. Wake
up at the top of the hill near the college. Lake Belle,
e Wakefield and his dad fished, was on the left side
wn; and on the other side, out past the new sub-
ions, there was a skating rink and a drive-in movie.
at arrangement, Wakefield thought. Even the name
e town was sensible. It was called Highview because,
u climbed up the campus water tower a little way,
ould see three counties.

course, some didn't like the town because it wasn't
nough for pro ball, or visiting groups like The
eb or The Electric Range. But Wakefield figured
f you couldn't live in Tahiti or the Arctic Circle,
might as well live in Kentucky. There was snow
e winter and hot days in the summer. And if you

18

could pick a town in Kentucky, Highview was better than some. Tag thought it might be better to live over in the mountains where the attendance officer couldn't find him—until he remembered the rattlesnakes.

Wakefield watched with envy as Tag went down the street until he seemed only a speck in the distance. Not having parents around, Tag never had to be home at certain times. He didn't have to get his homework if he didn't want to—most times he didn't want to—and he didn't have to go to bed until he was good and ready. Tag-Along Toomey, who wasn't nearly as responsible as Wake and not even quite as old, could manage his own life. Nobody told Tag-Along Toomey that he was too young for this or too old for that.

The houses Wakefield passed were set well back off the street with giant old maples in the front yards and a few swings still on the porches. There were wreaths on the broad front doors and decorations at the diamond-paned windows. Wakefield stalked on by, head down. He didn't notice that the Warrens were putting lights on their roof, or that the Irish setter he usually spoke to barked until he was out of sight.

It was useless to think about the Geronimo 300. His dad said firmly that a boy of nine was too young for a fancy rod. "Lose too much equipment." Of course that was at Lake Belle when he was just past nine. Now that he was almost ten . . . No—when his dad said anything "firmly," that was that. Imogene Cooke could probably wheedle a fly rod from her dad, but his dad just got more stubborn when people wheedled.

He kicked viciously at a half-melted, lopsided snowman, knocking chunks of snow down inside his boots. "It's a cinch," he said aloud, "that I can't ask Santa Claus for a Geronimo 300."

Old Mrs. Thornberry, who was walking toward Wake just then, stopped short, a puzzled look on her face. "I'll tell you what, Sonny. Why don't you ask old Santy for a wagon instead? Wouldn't that be nice? A little red wagon?"

CHAPTER

2

As soon as he opened the back door and stepped into the hall, Wakefield smelled cinnamon. That meant his mom was home and not at work. When the house smelled like lemon furniture polish, Aunt Glenna was there. (Aunt Glenna wasn't really any kin, but she'd been around the family so long, it seemed silly to call her "Mrs. MacGregor.")

There was one other person who took care of him and Sarah, and that was his dad, Thomas Quinn. This could be embarrassing sometimes; for example, when his mom taught evening classes and his dad was washing dishes and the doorbell rang. He'd go right to the door in his apron—not a butcher's apron—but a regular apron with long sashes and a heart-shaped pocket.

One time Wakefield asked his dad if he *had* to wear

the apron. Eddie Beard had just come by to trade base-ball cards, and knowing Eddie, the news that Mr. Quinn wore an apron would be all over school the next day.

"Do I have to wear an apron? Of course I do. These are my best pants." He was balancing a tower of ten glasses and inching it toward the dish cabinet.

"Okay, then, why doesn't Mom stay home and do the dishes? Eddie Beard's mother does. Mr. Beard wouldn't be caught dead wearing a lady's apron."

"Does Mrs. Beard run a thriving business like your mom?" (Mrs. Quinn owned a shop downtown, called "The Studio," where people came to make things out of clay.)

Wakefield shook his head.

"Then there's your answer." His dad pitched him a sponge. "Start wiping off counters while I do the sink."

Wakefield stared at the sponge. "But why *should* Mom run a business?"

"Why shouldn't she?"

He considered this at some length. His mom was smart enough; she knew about prime factors and multiples. She also understood the difference between *lie* and *lay,* which was something he never could get straight. But still he wasn't satisfied. "How come she *wants* to work?" he asked. (Wakefield seldom wanted to work.)

"Well, for two reasons, I think. One,"—his dad always talked like that: *one* and *two* and *A* and *B*—"she wants to save toward college for you and Sarah. Two, she has to. For her soul's sake."

"Her soul's sake?"

"You want to move that sponge back and forth?" His dad leaned back against the counter and wiped his hands on his apron. "Your mother's a little more than most people," he explained. "She has so much talent, so much energy inside her that it either gets bottled up or spills out. When it gets bottled up, look out! But if she's sharing her talents with other people, then she's happy. And when she's happy, we're happy. Right?"

"Right. But I still wish you wouldn't wear that apron when Eddie Beard comes."

"I'll try to remember," his dad promised solemnly; then he flipped Wakefield with the dish towel. "Now, let's raid the cookie jar. Your mom baked today; but I guess you already know that, don't you?"

It was baking day again. Man, what smells! His mom was so busy baking that she didn't notice the time; all he got for being late was a smile and a sample of almond crescents. These were his favorite cookies, soft and buttery, with nuts inside and powdered sugar on the outside.

23

He snitched two more.

Mrs. Quinn said "How was school?" and Wakefield said "Okay," which is what they always said.

"Old snow is brown and gray and ugly," he told her between cookies. He stood at the window watching the melting snow making puddles in his footprints.

"Well! For a boy starting his vacation you're not exactly Mr. Happy."

"Christmas is no fun without Santa Claus. All that business is for little kids. What else is there to be happy about?"

"Without Santa Claus?" she gasped and put a hand over her mouth. "Do you realize what you said?"

His mother was a big tease, but she probably did half-believe. She always made a big fuss over Christmas.

"Well, maybe *you're* not too old for Santa Claus, but I am." He turned to the steamy window again and wrote "Bah, humbug" on the glass. "I'm either too old, or I'm too young."

"Too young?" Mrs. Quinn looked up from her work and blew a strand of hair off her forehead, one of the few gray wisps tucked in among the black.

'I'm too young for a fly rod—ask Dad—even though I really need one."

"You don't *need* one; you *want* one. Big difference

there. What you really need is a trout stream. Where would you use a fly rod around here, Wakefield? There's not a trout in a hundred miles."

"I'd find a place."

As grumpy as Wakefield was, he still felt up to handling the beaters. Between licks of peppermint icing he complained: "This is going to be a stupid Christmas, nothing's any fun anymore. There's nothing to do."

Usually when he was dumb enough to gripe about not having anything to do, his mother *told* him: clean your room, sweep the porches, do your homework, feed Foo Cat. This time she looked at him thoughtfully.

"Wakefield, I've been so busy these last few years, I may not have noticed that you're growing up. My problem is that I still remember when you were two years old, and you saw your first escalator. I can still see that cute navy cap you wore and those little short pants. You stood there pointing up and shouting, 'Big stairs a-coming; big stairs a-coming.'"

Mrs. Quinn smiled dreamily, but not Wakefield. "Mom, I wish you'd stop telling that." *Short pants, for heaven's sake.*

"I know. I must stop seeing you as you were then and start seeing you as you are now. And right now I see that you're old enough to help me more than you've been

25

doing. Heaven knows I'll never get everything done by myself this Christmas. I've got to deliver Imogene's head by the twenty-third! (Mrs. Quinn had made Imogene in clay for Mrs. Cooke, who ordered it as a Christmas present for Mr. Cooke. Wakefield couldn't see how Imogene's dad could get excited over a present like that.)

"Your dad has some work for you, now that you're older. He wants you to help him with some sort of woodworking project." She slid another tray of cookies into the oven. "You should be thinking about what to get him for Christmas, you know. Oh my, there's a blue million things to do!"

"I suppose I could get him an ashtray. He might start smoking again."

"Wakefield!"

"He doesn't have to put ashes in it, Mom. He could use it on his desk for stamps and paper clips, and all that important junk we're not supposed to touch."

"Why not think about making him one? There's plenty of clay around."

Wakefield thought about it. In fact, he got so carried away with the idea that he ate three more cookies without realizing it.

He took the basement stairs two at a time and skidded into Mrs. Quinn's workroom. It was a comfortable, musty-smelling place. Crocks of wet clay covered with damp cloths stood on the floor. Crusted chisels and cutting tools were scattered around the tables, and over everything there was a powdery gray rust. On rainy days he used to sit here on an apple crate and watch his mom make people's heads with no eyeballs in them. He knew about clay all right.

"Look out, here comes Wakefield," he said, as he plunged his hands wrist deep into the squashy clay. He came up with a fat lump and threw it on the wedging board. "Take that, Mad Dog," he grunted, slamming down the clay a second time. He had to get the air bubbles out. If he didn't, they'd expand with the heat of the kiln and explode. Then, pow!—goodbye, ashtray.

He let the clay ooze in and out between his fingers for a while and listened to it splat against the board. Then he gave it a few last throws for fun, this time yelling, "Imogene Cooke!" Somehow the yelling and throwing put him in a good mood again. By the time he'd flattened out the clay with his mom's wide rolling pin, he was whistling.

"Anybody for cookies?" he asked, as he rolled the circle of clay over one hand and eased it into a pie pan. With a sharp knife he trimmed the edges. "How about a nice clay pie?" he asked, looking up again.

"I want some pie."

Wakefield jumped. It had been so quiet in the basement. It wouldn't be quiet now, not with his little sister Sarah around. Sarah never ever ran out of questions.

"I just have clay pie today," he said. "Want some?"

"You're silly, Wakefield. You want me to watch you?" Her big blue eyes stared hopefully.

Wakefield hesitated. Sarah, who was only five, was a pest. She never meant to, really, but she was always breaking his model cars or getting candy all over his homework papers. "Come on in," he said finally. "Only watch, don't help."

While Sarah sang day-school songs to him, he dipped his hands in water and smoothed the clay until it was even all over. The ashtray looked pretty sharp at this point, but it lacked a little something.

"You have to decorate it," Sarah explained.

"A fish in the center," Wakefield said.

"No, an owl. Owls are nice. Fish smell bad."

"Fish don't smell; they stink." Fish talk made him think of the Geronimo 300. For a little while he'd forgotten. "Oh man, do I ever want a fly rod."

"To catch flies?" Sarah asked.

Wakefield looked at her, hard, to see if she were teasing, but she was dead serious.

"No, bass and trout. Other fish, too, I guess."

"I'll buy you one for Christmas." When she nodded, her yellow curls bounced up and down. "I've saved eighty-two cents."

Wakefield rolled out another piece of clay—a skinny piece this time—and made two flat dents with a bottle cap for eyes. With a popsicle stick he pressed here and there for feathers. "You keep your eighty-two cents," he told Sarah, between feathers. "Fly rods cost lots of money."

"Then I'll tell Santa to bring you one. Or Daddy's probably rich. He could buy you one."

"He could, but he wouldn't. *When you're older,* he says. I imagine that means when I'm fifty or sixty."

All of a sudden the clay darkened, then grew light again. A shadow had passed behind him. Somebody must be looking through the back window. Imagination? Wakefield dragged a chair to the window and scrambled up, but there was nothing to see—only snow and sparrows.

He pasted the owl in the middle of the ashtray with his mom's slip. ("*Slip* is not what you think," he told Sarah. "It's a kind of liquid clay.") A hurried final smoothing, and while Sarah held the door open, he carried the finished product upstairs and into the kitchen.

"Did you get all the air bubbles out?" Mrs. Quinn asked. "You know it'll blow if you left even one bubble in."

"Wakefield the Great always gets the bubbles out."

"Then I think it is truly a remarkable piece of work." She put it on top of the cupboard to dry. "After you clean up your mess I want you to run an errand for me."

Great! Clean up your mess. When he got to be a parent, he'd never ever spoil the fun by saying "clean up your mess."

When he finished—he never wasted too much time cleaning—Mrs. Quinn was packing the cookies. He helped her arrange the sugar cookies, the Russian tea cakes, and the shortbread in foil-lined boxes. They tucked in the dark ones—the hermits and walnut squares and brownies—for contrast. The special ones, decorated with cherries and citron leaves, went on top. His mom put clear plastic wrap over the boxes and tied them each with a red bow. As a final touch, she slipped pieces of shiny green boxwood through the ribbons. The cookies looked good enough—well—to eat.

"Now, you take these cookies 'round to Mrs. Parker's, Aunt Helen's, and Old Peterson and your grandmother's." Mrs. Quinn loaded them carefully in the basket of his bike, and Wakefield rode off to make his deliveries.

He detoured around Mad Dog Hennessey's block. No use asking for trouble—not with twelve dozen cookies in the basket. His grandmother's house he left till last. He had his reasons. Sure enough, as soon as he mentioned what a big day he'd had and how pooped he was, his grandmother said he certainly needed a little something to perk him up.

"Do you think a little nap might help?" she asked.

He knew she was teasing. "I think hot chocolate would work faster."

"We could try that first and then see how you feel."

While his grandmother measured milk and sugar and cocoa, Wakefield brought up the subject of the fly rod. Usually Granny saw things his way, but this time was different.

"When I was a girl, I remember one fall—the trees don't seem to turn as yellow as they used to, do they?—anyway, a bunch of us young people went down to Harrods Creek. We packed a picnic lunch—that is, the girls did—and we all had cane poles. The boys dug red worms. Such a warm afternoon it was. We hit a croppie run and caught fish as fast as we could bait the hooks. There was this fellow who happened by, from Louisville, he said. He had on big high boots and a fancy hat with hooks hanging around the band. That man nearly whipped his arm off. I must stay he didn't give up easy. Didn't catch a thing all afternoon. We offered the poor man a pole and a can of worms, but he said no thanks, he only used artificial."

When his granny got going on the good old days, there was no stopping her. He was 100 percent certain now, that Granny wasn't going to put *Wakefield—fly rod* on her shopping list.

"Wakefield, you stick with that outfit of yours," she said. "Can't go wrong with a red worm and a number four hook and a good ol' reliable cane pole."

CHAPTER

3

That night Wakefield had a dream. Usually he didn't remember his dreams, but this one was so real that he sat up in bed right away. He'd been fishing a fine stretch of empty beach. It was very hot, the sun blazed down on his bare back, the sand was warm to his feet. All of a sudden he felt a tremendous tug on his line. His pole arched over until its tip touched the sand. "A tuna!" he remembered shouting. He tried to haul in his line, but the tuna had taken the hook and, in great powerful sweeps, was swimming for the open sea. Wakefield clung to the slender pole with all his might, but the giant fish towed him farther and farther away from shore. Suddenly there was a sharp crack. His cane pole had snapped into two jagged parts. The tuna flipped out of the water, shook away the hook, and swam on. Still grasping the stubby end of the pole, Wakefield felt the cold waves wash over him.

At that point he shrieked and woke himself up. (The covers had fallen off the foot of the bed, and an icy wind was billowing out the curtains by the dresser.) Even though he was fully awake now, he couldn't keep from thinking about that tuna. Such a great fish! *A cane pole, for goodness' sake!*

Was it fair that Imogene could get ice skates, and he couldn't get a fly rod? How come he had to wait until he was too old to enjoy a fly rod before he got one? He wanted it now, before he lost another tuna—even in his dreams. It wasn't as if the Geronimo 300 was a silly toy, like a doll that spits up, or like the space ship he had last year that was supposed to hit the moon, but always missed. The Geronimo 300 was a precision-built outfit that put fish in the frying pan.

By the time he had the window closed and the bed remade—sort of—he'd decided that he was going to have that rod in Sutcliff's window. He didn't know how exactly, he'd work that part out later. But Wakefield Kennedy Quinn was going to be the proud owner of the eight-foot Geronimo rod, the single-action reel, the monofilament leaders, and the two flies, hand-tied in Kenya, Africa. He felt so happy about his decision that

34

he popped right off to sleep. He didn't have any more dreams after that, at least that he could remember.

He thought about the rod from time to time the next day, though mostly he thought about *using* it, rather than *getting* it. His granny and his mom weren't going to buy him one—that was for sure—but there was still his dad. That night when the two of them went to the basement, he decided to ask him one more time—sometimes even parents change their minds. But he didn't mean to rush things; he meant to proceed very carefully.

"Do you think I might get a little work out of you, Son?" Mr. Quinn was poking around the shelves of his shop, looking for brushes.

Wakefield gave the question serious thought. "A little, maybe."

"In that case, why don't you paint this toy chest for your sister while I paint the little table and chairs? We'll be a pair of Picassos."

His dad was whistling. That was a good sign.

Wakefield had never painted anything that big in his whole life, but he said yes, anyway. It might be fun to be a Picasso. He spread newspaper on the floor and began to stir the red enamel, making an evil-looking whirlpool inside the can. While he swirled, his dad recited about a hundred verses of "The Shooting of Dan McGrew."

Along about verse seven, Wakefield started on the inside of the chest. As he stroked on the glossy red paint, a drip trickled down his arm, and he pretended that he was wounded by the "Crab That Ate Cincinnati."

After an hour of poetry and paint, Mr. Quinn announced it was time for a break. He and Wakefield sat under the stairs eating apples from the bushel basket. "Dad—" Wakefield swallowed a time or two and studied his apple. "Do you remember when I asked you about that, uh—fly rod?"

"Of course, I remember. I also remember saying that (A) it was an expensive outfit initially and that (B) the flies were expensive and that (C) youngsters lack the skill and the patience to manage the fly rod properly. They lose too much equipment."

His dad was a lawyer. He never forgot anything.

"My opinion hasn't changed, Wakefield. You'll just have to wait for what you want. Some people never learn that, you know."

There was no use arguing about it, Wake knew. Being a lawyer, his father knew how to argue back. So it was going to be up to Wakefield Kennedy Quinn to get his own Geronimo. But how? Aunt Glenna always said where there's a will, there's a way. What way? In the back of his *American Angler* magazine, he remembered, there were lots of money-making plans: *Raise Earth-worms at Home for Big Profits. Grow Mushrooms. Sell Friendship Corner greeting cards and watch your savings grow.*

He realized with a start that his dad had been talking to him. "Your mother tells me you've acquired twenty-five dollars. What about that?"

"That's class money. I have to buy an aquarium the day after Christmas." *How long would it take mushrooms to grow? Didn't they just sprout up over night?*

"That's quite a bit of money. Do you still have your tin box to keep it in?"

Wakefield nodded. *It was the wrong season for earthworms.*

"You haven't had a great record with possessions, you know. You lost your lunch money twice last week, your leather-palmed gloves, your library card—"

Wakefield interrupted before his dad ran out of breath. "This is different."

"It certainly is. The whole class is depending on you this time. Quite a responsibility."

"Responsibility." What an ugly word, Wakefield thought. It even sounded ugly. Some words had a nice sound—like *lollipop* and *double dribble* and *snicker-doodle.* But responsibility sounded as cold and hissing

37

as those notes Miss Booth put on his report card: "Wakefield does well on tests but must show more responsibility where homework is concerned."

"Now what did you have in mind for your mother for Christmas?" his dad said, getting up again. "You know how she appreciates anything handmade. Could you come up with something yourself?"

Before they finished painting, Wakefield had come up with a double idea. He hold his dad, "What I'd really like to do—that is, if I were older—is to make her a planter. She's been wanting one to set on the bookcase for those long trailing plants." *If the neighbors came in and saw the planter, maybe they'd give him orders. Last year Eddie Beard had sold six bricks that he'd painted up to use as doorstops.*

"Philodendron. Well, you're almost ten. Why not?"

They found a piece of cherry, and Wakefield sketched the dimensions on paper. Then, measuring carefully—his dad was very big on measuring—he marked off three equal pieces for the sides and the bottom, and two smaller ones for the ends. He used the power saw all by himself, while Mr. Quinn said to be careful fifty million times. His hand shook from the vibrations of the saw, and he could taste the sawdust, but, at last, the five neatly squared-off pieces were cut and stacked.

Suddenly, Mr. Quinn stopped reciting right in the middle of one of the corniest verses. He put his finger to his lips and pointed toward the basement window. "Did you hear something?" he whispered.

He and Wakefield both listened, straining to hear over the sounds of the house. The furnace whirred, water dripped from the tap, the television upstairs droned on and on. Wakefield could hear himself breathing.

"I suppose I was mistaken," Mr. Quinn said. "I had a strong sensation that we were being watched. Let's call it a day. I'm so tired that I'm hearing things." He checked the window latches while Wakefield swept up.

"We'll have to put in an hour or two every night, if we hope to get finished by Christmas." Mr. Quinn switched off the power saw and hung his tools back on the pegboard rack. "I'll teach you 'The Cremation of Sam McGee' while we work."

It was a cinch that the planter business was not for him, Wakefield decided. He figured he'd be pretty sick of Sam McGee by the time he made enough planters to finance the Geronimo 300.

CHAPTER

4

The next morning when Wakefield came down to breakfast, there wasn't any. Instead there was a note propped against the sugar bowl: "You're on your own. Have gone to museum and guild shop and library to deliver sculpture. Sarah is at Granny's. Think you can make breakfast and hold down the fort? Signed: The Wicked Witch of the West."

That was his mom, of course. She always signed crazy names to her notes. There was cereal and juice and toast without even cooking, but he decided on something more substantial: a slice of chocolate cake, a glass of instant iced tea, and spaghetti from last night's dinner. Miss Booth would probably drop her teeth over such a meal—she was very big on the Basic Four—and that made his food taste even better.

He had no big plans for the morning—other than

ambling around the town to see what was going on—but twenty minutes after breakfast he found himself in front of Sutcliff's Sporting Goods. The rod was still there, and the reel with its adjustable drag and push-button release. The top quality fly line nestled under the branches of Mr. Sutcliff's tree, and the flies in their plastic compartments winked red and green from the reflections of the Christmas lights. But something was different. There was a cardboard sign standing in the middle of the display. At the top of the sign, the original price, $39.95, had been crossed out, and on the bottom of the sign was printed:

LAST ONE IN STOCK—$24.95—NO RETURNS.

The last one in stock! The last Geronimo 300! Wakefield was horrified. There was no time for growing mushrooms or selling Friendship Corner greeting cards. There was no time for making planters. The next person who walked by Sutcliff's would snap up that outfit in nothing flat. And there would never ever be another bargain like the Geronimo, with the hand-tied flies made in Kenya, Africa, and the monofilament leaders and the little plastic worm.

Mr. Sutcliff came to the door and called out: "Could I help you with anything? Looking for something to buy your dad?"

41

"This rod and reel," Wakefield said. "The sign says last one in stock."

"Yep, clearing out my inventory. Gonna close up shop for a month and go to Florida. Clear to the Keys. Deep-sea fishing. Marlin, sailfish, maybe tuna. Mighty fine rod there, a medium fast action, I'd say. Can't go wrong with quality."

"Tuna, you say?"

"Yep, got a 150-pound yellowfin last year, trolling. 'Course some said it was luck, which may be true, but it takes skill, too, and sound equipment."

Wakefield looked at the rod again. If it could talk, he thought, it would be saying, "Take me home."

"Now, some people don't appreciate good equipment," Mr. Sutcliff was saying, "Don't keep it in shape, never oil it, never clean it after a trip. Might as well be fishing with a cane pole and a cork, I always say."

A cold blast of air sent Mr. Sutcliff scurrying in. He yelled as he left, "Come on in if you see anything you want. Got a special on golf balls. Your dad could use some of those come spring. He lost enough last fall." He was laughing as the door closed.

Suddenly the aquarium money, which Wakefield had neglected to take out of his pocket and put away, began to make an uncomfortable bulge under his parka. He could feel the fold of bills, the quarters, the dime, the nickel, and each of the two pennies. It occurred to him in a flash that he didn't really need that money until the twenty-sixth of December. But the rod was for sale now. The very last rod.

He thought fast. His Arizona grandmother always sent him ten dollars for Christmas, his Uncle Ernie in the army sent five. That was fifteen dollars right there! There was probably five dollars in his dime bank at home, maybe even six or seven. Seven and fifteen made twenty-two. He wouldn't need but three more dollars for the aquarium, and anybody could round up three dollars. One time he'd found a dollar in a library book, and a quarter once, right out in the middle of the sidewalk.

He ran into Sutcliff's.

"Made up your mind, yet?" Mr. Sutcliff had ambled in from the storeroom.

"The fly outfit," Wakefield said, a little out of breath. Mr. Sutcliff went to remove it from the window. "I've just got $24.67. That makes me—" Wakefield subtracted in his head—"twenty-eight cents short. Could I buy on credit and pay you the twenty-eight cents when I get my allowance? That's this weekend."

"I'll be long gone by then. Leaving day after tomorrow." Mr. Sutcliff was looking at the fishing gear. Wakefield was looking at the floor.

"Tell you what," the shop owner said. "You can see that the lure box here has a little crack in the corner. I'll knock off the twenty-eight cents, if you'll take it as is."

Wakefield nodded, too relieved to say anything. Mr. Sutcliff found a box for the purchases and wrapped it in brown store-paper.

"Yessiree, your dad's gonna be proud of this little outfit. None better." Mr. Sutcliff rang up the sale while Wake counted out his money. Wake didn't bother telling Mr. Sutcliff that the rod was for him, not his dad. Mr. Sutcliff was the kind of man who'd come right out and tell you not to buy things, if he thought they weren't suitable. At this point, when the rod was almost in his hands, Wakefield didn't care to hear one more time that he was too young to handle a fly rod.

Mr. Sutcliff handed him the package and wished him merry Christmas, and Wake said, "Thanks and happy New Year," and he was out on the street.

The package was big, so big that anybody who saw him carrying it had to think it was important. Wakefield walked slowly, stopping to look at himself in shop windows, nodding politely to people who eyed his bulky package. A lady waiting for a bus on the corner said,

"My, that's almost as big as you are. Is that a Christmas present?"

"In a way," Wake said. "I gave it to myself. It's a fishing pole." He didn't say "three-and-a-half-ounce fly rod" and "single-action reel," because he thought she might not know about an advanced sport like fly fishing.

Her bus came then, but she mouthed something at the window, which looked like, "Get that big one!"

He decided to hurry on home and examine the Geronimo 300, piece by piece. He'd really never held the rod yet, gotten the feel of the thing.

Upstairs in his room, he wound on the line, tied on a leader, and attached the hook with a jam knot. He'd watched his dad do these things, but still it wasn't as easy as his dad made it seem. He had to make two or three tries at his clinch knot before he got his Royal Coachman fastened securely. Now he was ready to go.

Even with the twelve-foot ceilings in the old house, he had sense enough to know that he couldn't manage an overhand cast, but if he stood at the end of the long narrow hall that faced his room, he could certainly do a side-arm. The side-arm cast would be handy for getting in low under overhanging trees, the very place where the really big bass like to hide.

He set his empty waste can in the door of his room

and from the far end of the hall, stripped off some line, flexed his pole, and "ping," the Royal Coachman hit the side of the can. He tried a second cast and, bull's-eye, right inside the can. *Who said he was too young to manage a fly rod!* He set the waste can farther back and leaned out over the stair rail to try an angle shot. "Zing." He waited, but there was no ping after the zing.

The fly was nowhere in sight. Impossible! He turned the waste can upside and shook it, but there just wasn't any fly. He looked to the left and right and finally as a last resort, straight up. It was hard to believe, but there was his line, stretched taut, angling toward the ceiling and then into his room. He followed it across his bed and around his coatrack and up past the bookcase to the top of his window. And there was his Coachman, all right. Only the tiniest tip of it showed; the rest was imbedded in the heavy monkscloth curtains.

He stacked five encyclopedias on his chair and stood on top of them, but he still couldn't quite reach the tail of the fly. He made grabs at it, turning and twisting the line and jiggling the curtains, but the sharp barb stayed firmly in place.

The front door creaked open in the downstairs hall, and Sarah came bounding in, talking a mile a minute. Mrs. Quinn was already calling at the foot of the stairs:

"Wakefield, are you up there?"

He made one last grab at the Coachman, and rod and fly and curtains, still firmly connected, fell to the floor.

"Wakefield?"

"Be right down," he tried to make his voice cheery.

Working quickly, he rolled the curtains around the rod and the tangled loops of line, and stuffed the whole thing into his closet. With his foot, he shoved the wrappings and box under his bed, pulling the bedspread to the floor to hide the evidence. He took a deep breath then, slowed his pace, and tried to whistle as he walked downstairs.

"Wakefield"—his mother was not easily upset, but this time her voice didn't sound too friendly—"Why didn't you wash your breakfast dishes? You're ten years old now; I shouldn't have to clean up after you."

"Nine years old. I'm going to get those dishes, mom. I just haven't had time yet."

Oh? What were you doing?"

Wakefield tried to think. He cracked his knuckles and tapped his foot, but not a single brilliant idea came to him. Finally, he said, not looking at his mother, "Oh, just messing around."

"Evidently," she snapped, with a glance at the spaghetti wiggles on the table.

To Wakefield's relief, she reached for her old smock that hung beside the basement door. That meant she'd be working on old Imogene for a couple of hours. Maybe he could get his room back to rights unnoticed.

After she'd disappeared down the steps, Wakefield took great care in cleaning up the kitchen. He even polished the handle on the refrigerator and watered the

ivy. But despite his good work, he felt uncomfortable. For one thing, he wasn't used to sidestepping his mother's questions. Oh, he might forget to mention a bad spelling grade now and then, but when she asked him something right out, he'd always told the 90 percent truth.

For the first time, it occurred to him that he had his fly rod, but what could he do with it? He couldn't show

it to his dad—that was for certain! Or his friends, somebody would be sure to rat on him. His sister couldn't
keep a secret even if she wanted to and tried very hard.

The Geronimo 300 was going to be a problem, all
right.

CHAPTER

5

The next few days Wakefield worked very hard on his Christmas projects. Tag stopped by three or four times a day, but Wake was too busy to play outside. Tag would sit on the steps for a while, bouncing a ball or blowing big pink balloons with his bubble gum. Finally, he'd give up and trudge back down the hill.

Mrs. Quinn worried that Wakefield was working *too* hard. From time to time she'd stare at him and feel his forehead. "Would you like me to beat up an egg in some milk for you?" she'd say. "You're not yourself."

Wakefield always insisted that he was okay, and that he definitely wouldn't like an egg in milk.

"You're not staying up late to watch those horror movies on TV?"

"No, really I'm not. I'm fine." He'd dart down to the

51

workroom then, before his mother could think up more questions. It was a strange thing, but the nicer his mom was to him, the more miserable he felt. If the government ever needed anyone to question spies, his mother'd be the one!

He'd spoken truthfully about not watching TV, but he *had* been losing sleep. Every night, when he was sure the family was asleep, he shut himself in the closet. There, by the beam of his flashlight, he untangled fishing line. The first night he worked the hook out of the material and rehung his curtains. There were some loose threads hanging and a small tear, but he arranged the folds so that the damage was almost hidden. As he was getting down off the chair to admire his work, somehow he caught his foot in a light cord. The desk lamp crashed to the floor. It clattered as it rolled, and a second later the light bulb shattered. He froze.

His dad growled from down the hall: "Drat that cat! Didn't you put him out, Martha?"

A sleepy voice answered, "Didn't you?" and nothing else happened.

Other nights he worked more silently. He picked at knots with a needle, tracing down loops and snarls, hanging circles of line over his shoulders, and then winding them around the door knob. One night, when he was almost finished, Foo Cat sneaked up, grabbed the line and pounced under the bed with it. And he couldn't even scream at Foo; he had to maintain strict silence.

The good thing about working during the day, besides avoiding his mom, was that it took his mind off other things. Wakefield observed that if you really got interested in a project, if you really worked hard, that's all you could think about. You forgot to ask yourself what would happen if your dad found out you spent money that didn't belong to you, even though you fully intended to pay it back. Or what would happen if Aunt Glenna got a sudden whim to clean out closets. Or how in the world you could use a fly rod you weren't even supposed to own.

The ashtray had required several afternoons' work. When it had dried thoroughly, Wakefield had to sand the rough edges with fine sandpaper. At this stage, the clay was called "greenware," according to his mom, and was very fragile. By concentrating, he'd managed to sand and sponge off the clay dust without demolishing the whole works. The ashtray was now ready to be fired.

The cherry planter looked great, especially after he'd lined it with copper, which was tricky business. (If you wanted to see how sharp those metal edges were, all you had to do was count the adhesive strips on his fingers.)

Mr. Quinn had insisted that Wakefield sand the planter between coats of varnish, which was about as exciting as the multiplication table, but the finish was beginning to be as smooth as a dog's nose.

Wednesday afternoon late, Mr. Quinn came down to repair one of Sarah's toys and to check Wakefield's progress. They worked together silently until his dad came to a stopping point. "I think I'm going to have to bring a radio down here, Wakefield. You don't talk any more. Anything the matter?"

Wakefield shook his head. (Usually his dad complained about too much noise instead of not enough.)

"Something on your mind?" Mr. Quinn asked.

"No."

"A secret, maybe?"

"Sort of." Wakefield didn't look at his dad.

"Well, in that case I won't pry. A person has a right to his secrets around Christmas." He looked at his watch and turned off the drill. "It's Wednesday night and the stores close early. We need fine-grained sandpaper."

As they were hurrying toward the car, Mrs. Quinn called out, "Bring home supper. I can't stop." She was making some kind of a box stand for Imogene's head. (Privately, Wakefield thought Imogene would look better if the box were *over* her head instead of under it.)

54

His dad let him out in front of the shopping center and drove on to pick up some fish and chips, still grumbling about not ever having a decent meal. (For several days Mrs. Quinn had been too busy at The Studio to cook.) Wakefield thought the meals all week had been super: hamburgers, chicken in a basket, pizzas, TV dinners. What could be better?

He bought the sandpaper in the hardware store. Usually he got so interested in the bins of nails and racks of tools that he forgot what he came for. With his dad in a black mood, though, Wakefield figured he'd better be ready to hop in the car the minute it pulled to a stop. Still counting his change, he rushed right past the riding lawnmowers and the wheel toy display and out onto the sidewalk—and right into Mad Dog Hennessey.

"Well"—Mad Dog put his big beefy hands on his hips —"has little Wakey put up his Twismas twee yet?"

"Aw, come off it, Mad Dog. I'm in a hurry."

"Oh? Gotta write to Santy Claus?" Mad Dog threw back his head and laughed at how clever he was.

"Listen, Mad Dog, let me by. My dad's coming for me, and I have to be ready."

"If you want by, you'll have to fight me." He spread his arms and legs apart blocking Wake from the curb. Then he began to chant in a simpering little voice:

"Wakey's gotta twim his Twismas twee; Wakey's gotta twim his Twismas twee."

Suddenly Mad Dog stopped, a stricken look on his face. He clutched his backside and began to jump up and down and howl.

"Wakefield!" he shrieked, "you shot me with a bean-shooter, I know you did."

"How could I? I'm standing right in front of you."

Hennessey might be the strongest boy in sixth grade, but he wasn't the brightest.

Mad Dog began to look around frantically. He rushed over to a stack of crates in front of the hardware store and shoved them aside with his foot. He looked behind parked cars and even in the trash can at the curb. He charged off like a mad bull to check the side of the building. About halfway there, he stopped short and sucked in his breath. Somebody had taken another shot at him and hit the bull's-eye again.

Wakefield doubled up with laughter. Mad Dog was shaking his fist and clutching the seat of his pants. He looked like a balloon ready to pop; he was all red in the face, and his cheeks were pooched out like a puff adder's. Finally Wakefield laughed so hard he had to hold to the lamp post for support. Tears of laughter were streaming down his cheeks when his dad drove up. As they pulled away from the curb, Mad Dog came running after the car yelling, "I'll get you for this, Wakefield, I'll get you."

His dad raised an eyebrow. "Good to hear you laugh. What's the joke?" Even his dad had to laugh when he heard the story. He laughed so much, that by the time they got home he'd stopped grumbling about fish and chips from the Sea Castle. He was singing sea chantys and calling everybody Matey and Cap'n and Wakefield's mother "a pretty enough lass for a seafarin' man."

Halfway through dinner his mother jumped up, nearly knocking over her chair. (Wakefield supposed she was old enough to do that without getting fussed at.) "I almost forgot," she said. "A package came while you were gone."

"Is it big?" Sarah asked. "Humongous?" *Humongous* was Sarah's favorite word.

"Is it ever!" Mrs. Quinn brought the package to the table, and Wakefield stopped eating, a french fry still dangling from his mouth.

"Wakefield, really!" his dad said.

While Mrs. Quinn clipped the string, Wakefield swallowed hard. He'd recognized his Arizona grandmother's spidery writing on the brown paper. Something was wrong. Granny Quinn never sent packages at Christmas.

Lying inside the box on top of folds of tissue paper was a Christmas card with a note. Mrs. Quinn read it aloud.

Dear Children: (*that meant his mom and dad*)

I usually send the grandchildren a check for Christmas because, living so far, I can't keep up with their sizes in sweaters or their tastes in toys. But this year I decided to make each of them a quilt, something for them to keep, something they won't outgrow. The Flower Garden is for little Sarah—there are bits and pieces of her dresses there which she will recognize—and the Star is for Wakefield. I thought he might fancy the geometric pattern. The Double Wedding Ring is for you and Martha.

Love and Merry Christmas,

Granny Quinn

Excitement filled the room. Mother was exclaiming, "Look, Tom. All those tiny stitches." Sarah was hugging her Flower Garden and jumping up and down. "My

59

very own quilt! My very own grandmother!" Mr. Quinn was crawling around the Double Wedding Ring, which was now spread over newspapers on the floor. "Isn't that piece—over there in the bottom corner—didn't you have a dress like that the first year we were married?"

Mrs. Quinn was crying now. "Oh, Tom," she kept saying, "Think of the hours that went into these quilts. You just don't get handcrafted work like this anymore."

Wakefield hadn't moved. He was stunned. He had this terrible feeling, the same kind he had before an oral report in English. His stomach had drawn itself into a hard fist and was pushing up toward his throat. There was no ten dollars! There wasn't going to *be* any ten dollars!

He scraped his chair away from the table and ran upstairs to his room.

CHAPTER

6

Later on that evening Mrs. Quinn came to Wakefield's room. She tapped gently on the door, but Wake turned over and hid his face in the pillow. The door squeaked open. "Are you asleep?" she said. "We're concerned about you." Wakefield didn't move a muscle. Mrs. Quinn stood over him for a moment, sighed, then tiptoed away.

After the house was quiet for the night, Wakefield eased carefully out of bed, took his bank and a nail file from the chest, and padded over to the closet. He crumbled up a couple of sweat shirts to mask the clinking, then loosened the screws on the bottom of the bank with the file, and spilled out the dimes. Counting very carefully, he arranged them in stacks of ten. After four stacks he knew there weren't going to be seven stacks, not even six. There were five and a half stacks—exactly five dollars and fifty cents. And that included every cent of his December allowance. He stared at the stacks, re-arranged them a few times, then placed them carefully in a cigar box on the closet shelf.

In the pocket of his parka, he found a small spiral notebook with a few sheets that didn't have tic-tac-toe crosses on them. On one clean page he wrote, MONEY NEEDED—$24.67. On the opposite page he wrote, MONEY ON HAND—$5.50. He subtracted on a scratch sheet, drew a line through the $24.67 and wrote $19.17.

Nineteen dollars by December 26! No, nineteen dollars *and seventeen cents*. He decided that maybe one of his problems was that he was too optimistic. He'd counted on Granny Quinn's ten dollars, which didn't come, and now he'd just thrown away that seventeen cents —in his mind, anyway—and those extra pennies might be very important. As Aunt Glenna said, "A bird in the hand is worth two in the bush." Of course, there was the five dollars that Uncle Ernie always sent; it was safe to count on that. It was a cinch that Uncle Ernie wasn't going to make a quilt.

The next morning he was up early. He stood at the counter and ate a bowl of cereal, stuffed cookies in both pockets, and scribbled a note to Aunt Glenna: *I'm out.*

Will be back. He decided not to be too specific, or she'd come after him with a bottle of vitamin pills in one hand and a bowl of milk toast in the other. She might even bring him home. Aunt Glenna worried about his health a lot.

He took the shovel from the garage and set out to look for work. The big snow had fallen a week before. There'd been light snow flurries since, but most of the walks were clear, except for a few scattered icy patches. Over on Walnut, though, he found a real challenge. Mrs. Montgomery was really snowed in.

"Indeed I do want my walk cleared," she said. "Claude and I were just talking about it this morning." (Claude was her parakeet.) "My nephew was supposed to come last Thursday, but oh my, he's so irresponsible. I told Claude I just didn't know what to do about that boy."

All morning Wakefield scooped up snow, tossed it to the side, moved up a half-foot. He fell into a routine—scoop, lift, throw, and down—which made the work a little easier. Still his arm muscles ached, and there were blisters under his gloves. Usually he liked to examine cuts and scratches and wounds, but today he didn't dare. If the blisters looked really gross, he might be tempted to quit.

As he finished—he could hardly believe that the noon

whistle was blowing—Mrs. Montgomery invited him in and gave him hot chocolate while she looked for her purse. "Claude, did you see where I put my pocketbook?"

Claude chirped.

"Ah yes," she said. "Exactly. On top of the china cabinet."

Wakefield ate his cookies with the chocolate, at least what he could dig out of his pockets; they were pretty badly crumbled. Finally Mrs. Montgomery came back with three one dollar bills and two quarters. "Claude and I are very pleased with your work," she said. "We'll be happy to recommend you." Wakefield said thank you, nodded to Claude, and left. All the time he'd been subtracting in his head. He came up with $15.67—MONEY NEEDED. If he could get the figure closer to ten dollars he'd feel better about it.

He took a shortcut home and came across another snowy walk. He almost wished he hadn't seen it. He stood for some time looking toward the house, trying to figure out how many scoops there were from him to the porch. A lot, he decided. But there was no way around it, he had to ask for work. Maybe—just maybe—nobody would be at home.

There was. A high school girl came to the door, listened to him while she cracked her gum, and left to check with her mother. When she came back again, she had on her coat and was pulling on her gloves.

"Mom said okay, but you better do a good job or she won't pay you." She glared at Wakefield, then pushed by him, and slouched on down the street.

Wakefield wanted to walk right off the job before he even started. He didn't care for that girl one bit; she reminded him of Imogene Cooke. But he couldn't leave. He needed the money, and there just weren't that many snowy walks in Highview.

While he worked, he said his times tables to himself, counted backwards, and tried all the tricks he could think of to make the work go faster. He made himself stop looking at the end of the walk—the finish line. Two boys from Six-B came by and wanted him to go skating with them out at Scully's Pond; a lot of the kids were out there. Tag came by, too; he was on his way to the store to sell soft drink empties. He offered to keep Wake company, but Wake got so busy he forgot to talk, and Tag soon drifted off.

When he finished and had gone back over a spot or two just to make sure, he rang the bell. A stern-looking lady, still in her bathrobe, came to the door and frowned out at him. "Yes?" she said.

"I've finished your walks," Wakefield answered.

"I didn't want no walks done." The door started to close.

"But your girl said—"

"I don't know what Marybelle said. Can't believe half she says anyway. All I know is that you woke me up."

"But I *did* your walks." Wakefield bit his lip; he was so tired.

"Tough, kid. Next time you'd better ask the lady of the house. I've got no money to hire people to shovel snow. Marybelle's supposed to clear them walks."

The door closed completely and the lock clicked.

Wakefield wanted to throw all the snow back on top of the walks, but he couldn't lift one more shovelful. He trudged on home.

Aunt Glenna exploded when he came in. Her hearty face with its round cheeks was almost as red as her hair. "Where have you been? You scared me out of my wits, Wakefield. Sarah and I looked all over, and then I called your dad. He drove downtown and out to Scully's Pond."

Wakefield stared at her dully.

"You're sick. I knew you would be, going off like that with no muffler. An ounce of prevention is worth a pound of cure, I always say." Aunt Glenna's tone softened. "Poor duck. You're so wet and cold. Get out of those damp things and into your pajamas—the long-sleeved fuzzy ones you don't like. Then right into bed."

He hadn't had an afternoon nap since first grade. The fuzzy pajamas felt warm and snuggly, and Aunt Glenna brought him a hot water bottle for his feet. She gave him an extra blanket and tucked him in firmly, and that's the last thing he remembered until morning.

CHAPTER

7

Wakefield made short work of getting dressed the next day. His room was still chilly—old houses warm up slowly—so he scooped up his jeans and sweat shirt and dashed to the warm air register to dress. Voices from the kitchen below came up through the duct loud and clear. (He didn't exactly *try* to eavesdrop, but when you're standing over an echo chamber, what can you do?) His mother was saying: "Something is definitely wrong with the boy. He avoids me—he's always skittering down to the workshop; he won't look at me; he doesn't even talk."

Mr. Quinn spoke: "He's the same with me. I've asked him several times about his long silences. He simply denies them or changes the subject. Do you think we ought to have Dr. Giesel take a look at him?"

"I don't know, Tom. He does seem tired all the time,

and he yawns a lot. I think there's something worrying him, though."

"Like what?"

"I wish I knew. He didn't even look at the quilt his grandmother sent; that's not like him. And yesterday he left without telling us where he was going, or why. Glenna said he was thoroughly exhausted when he came in."

Mr. Quinn's voice grew a little louder and a lot sterner. "Wakefield understands that we must know where he is at all times. We have very few rules around this house. It does seem that he could remember the most important one." (Mr. Quinn was evidently stirring his coffee. Wakefield could hear the spoon clink against the cup.) The clinking got faster and louder. "If he stays in for the rest of the day, he might remember to inform us the next time he decides to wander."

"Perhaps"—Mrs. Quinn seemed to be thinking aloud —"perhaps we shouldn't punish him, Tom. I think his behavior is partly my fault."

"How's that?"

"It's possible that he resents my being at The Studio so much lately. Maybe there are things he wants to tell me, and I'm not here to be told."

"Glenna's here," Mr. Quinn said. "And Sarah's happy

as a lark. Why wouldn't she be as glum as Wakefield if your work were the cause of the problem?"

"I don't know. Perhaps it's the age difference. But if things get worse, I may put The Studio up for sale."

"Martha, I think you're making too much of this."

"We'll see." It was quiet for a few moments. Wakefield figured his mother must be thinking hard. "I intend to spend some time with him this morning," she said. "Can you get home early this afternoon? Maybe you could talk to him again."

"I'll check my schedule." There was a pause while pages flipped in Mr. Quinn's appointment book. "You're probably right about not punishing the boy. I won't confine him to the house this time. Maybe he needs *at*tention rather than *de*tention.

Somebody had switched on the kitchen radio. The news blared out, and Wakefield could no longer hear anything more than a low rumble of conversation. He didn't want to hear any more. He'd heard quite enough.

What a pickle he was in! Now he had his mom and dad all upset, as well as himself. When he could add that $15.67 to the cigar box, nobody would have anything to worry about. Until that time, the thing to do was to make a special effort to be cheerful and chatty. He'd have to be so cheerful that his mom wouldn't want to quit her job. (He really didn't want her to get her talents all bottled up.) He also wanted his dad to act natural again. It was great not having to stay in the house all day. But going unpunished made him feel uneasy. He felt as though he were waiting for the front hall clock to chime. It had been broken for some time and never chimed as much as it was supposed to. When it was three o'clock it struck twice, and everybody kept listening for the other chime.

Today he must try very hard to talk to his mother.

She was trying just as hard to talk to him, he decided later. All morning she entertained him, just as if he were a guest in the house, and she were the hostess. She kept offering him snacks and inquiring about his friends and asking him if there wasn't something special he'd like to do. What he really wanted to do was to be out making money, and what his mom probably wanted to do was work on Imogene. But there they sat, yakking away like two magpies. It was all very creepy.

While they talked, his mom was rummaging through the desk drawers for last year's Christmas card list, stopping now and then to read an old newspaper clipping aloud or the backs of picture post cards. "You know," she said—she snapped her fingers as though she'd thought of a great idea—"you're getting too old to be lumped with the *and family* on our greeting cards. You should make your own cards."

He nodded, ready to go along with any suggestion.

"You can make a potato print, can't you? Didn't you learn that in art?"

He nodded again.

"Potatoes in the cabinet next to the refrigerator." She hesitated a moment. "Don't forget to —"

"I know. Put down plenty of newspapers."

His mother was prepared to go on into the playroom with him, but he explained how he liked to work alone. Sarah was around, now, to keep him company, and he surely would call if he needed any help. His mother finally went downstairs to work, but she didn't seem too happy about it.

Ignoring "helpful" suggestions from Sarah, he sketched several designs: a bell, a candle, and a Santa that looked like Dopey of the Seven Dwarfs. Finally, he chose a holly leaf and berries. He cut the big potato in half longways and sketched the leaf on one half, the berries on the other.

Then with a sharp knife he cut away the part of the potato around the leaf, leaving the leaf raised. (From time to time his mom peeked in the door and told him to "be careful—be careful—be careful.") Cutting around the holly berries was harder because they were small and curved. His hands were stiff and had blisters from the snow shoveling, which didn't help any, but the knife slipped only once, and he lost just two berries.

Next, he poured two saucers of tempera, one of red and one of green, which had to be protected from Sarah. She was jumping up and down with excitement. "Wakefield, can I paint? Can I paint?"

"You mean *may* I paint. No."

She looked so woebegone that he had to change his mind. "Put down plenty of newspapers," he told her.

He dipped the leaf in green paint and tried stamping it on the newspaper. Then he tried the berries, and it all looked great. He was ready for the real thing.

Sarah was working very hard, too. Her eyebrows drew together in a frown, and she gripped her brush with all her might. The card she'd made on old tablet paper didn't look half bad. In fact, it looked like some of the modern art he had seen when he went to the museum with his mother—kind of carefree. However, she'd also printed both her knees and was starting in on the cat.

"Tell you what, Sarah"—Wakefield grabbed her paint brush before it hit the carpet—"Why don't you help me make my cards now? Fold these white pieces of paper exactly in half. Are your hands clean?"

Wakefield printed cards for a couple of hours. First he put the leaf in the middle and the berries to one side. Then he experimented, making three or four leaves overlapping and a border of the berries. Finally, he had twenty-five good ones. Sarah took all the not-so-goods and was thrilled with them (it didn't take much to send Sarah into a spin). He signed his name inside and addressed one to every boy in his class, his boy cousins, and his pen pal in Utah. Mrs. Quinn kept one to stand on the mantel.

Cleaning up the mess took almost as much time as printing the cards. (Wakefield was really not the neatest boy in the world, and he did want to make a good impression on his mom.) The minute he was finished, he grabbed his coat and ran to mail his cards. He knew if he didn't leave quickly, somebody would remind him to wear gloves and all sorts of scratchy things. The walk down to the post office was bracing. The air was crisp and smelled of Christmas baking and wood fires. The sidewalks were coated with ice, and he slid most of the way.

He took a good look at Tag's house when he passed it (Tag lived down behind the post office). It was patched on the outside with sheets of tin, and there was cardboard at the windows and a crazy chimney tilting to one side.

The whole house was no bigger than the Quinns' living room. Wake thought it might be a nice camping shack in the summer, but he wasn't too sure about living there in the winter. There were big cracks in the siding that could get rather breezy in cold weather. For once, Tag wasn't around.

On the way back he passed Sutcliff's Sporting Goods. There was a sign on the door: *GONE FISHING.*

When he came home, he discovered that his mom had thawed the gingerbread men. With her work at The Studio, she didn't have time to cook each day, so she went on what she called "baking binges." Over the Thanksgiving holidays, the whole family had helped make the gingerbread men, the stollen, and nut cakes, and the cookie doughs, all of which—sad as it was at the time—went into the freezer. Now, day by day, the goodies appeared again.

"Let's decorate the gingerbread," his mom said. His mom couldn't bear to look at a naked cookie. She decorated everything in sight, which was all right with Wakefield.

"Do you want to ask Tag over to help?" Mrs. Quinn made a face when she said "Tag." She wasn't too keen on nicknames. "You don't play with your friends these days."

"Not at home. I just passed his house," Wakefield was happy to report.

That was some fun! There were three kinds of squirt icing and colored sprinkles and silver dragees and gum drops and anything you could think of to decorate with and eat. His dad came home in the middle of it all, squirted the icing can the wrong way and got it right in the face.

Wakefield decided that it was probably time for his dad to take over the business of "giving Wakefield some attention." Sure enough, as soon as everybody stopped laughing and the icing was wiped away, his dad asked, "What kind of lumberjack are you, Wakefield?"

"Just about the greatest," Wake answered. He made his voice sound happy. The sooner his parents thought everything was a-okay, the sooner he could get on with the business of earning $15.67.

"Then you're the man I'm looking for. We're going to cut the mightiest pine in McGinty's woods. That is, if you haven't left my ax out again."

"Who, me?" Wakefield planned to check secretly, just to make sure.

It was a great afternoon. The wind was biting cold, and Wakefield's breath made balloons of frost in the air. A covey of quail whirred up in his path, and fifty million rabbits jumped all around him. The ground was crunchy as they walked, and ice cakes floated in the creek.

Finally, on the farthest hill, they found two perfect trees. Wakefield couldn't decide between the two, so Mr. Quinn said, "Cut 'em both! We can use the smaller tree in the playroom. You'll have to supervise it, of course."

Each took a turn at the ax, and Wakefield yelled, "Timber!" as each pine crashed to the ground.

The trees had to be dragged to the car and lashed on top with clothesline. When the last knot was tied, Mr. Quinn made an announcement: "Next year, Wakefield, we're not going to be so particular. We're going to cut any tree in sight of the car."

"But Dad, *haste makes waste,* and *a thing worth doing at all is worth doing well.* Isn't that what Aunt Glenna always says?" Wakefield was laughing so hard he popped the bottom button on his parka.

"I know a bright boy who is *not* going to get the last cookie," said Mr. Quinn. They were sitting on a log, eating the snack Mrs. Quinn had packed for them. Wakefield had a thermos of chocolate and his dad had coffee.

"Is there anything you need to tell me, Wakefield?" His dad was drawing pictures in the snow with a stick. "Be glad to listen, you know."

"Nothing at all," Wakefield answered brightly. "Except that I'm having a fine time today. I really am."

His dad shrugged his shoulders and sighed. After a few minutes of uncomfortable silence, his dad got up. They scattered the crumbs for the few brown birds who were wintering in the field, and left.

When they got home, Mrs. Quinn was clearing out the cupboards in the kitchen to make room for party supplies. There were cartons of soft drink empties all around her feet. Wakefield, remembering Tag and his refund money, ask his mom, "Want me to get those cartons out of your way?"

"Wakefield, if you'll rescue me from all this, you can keep the money. I never saw so much clutter."

The man at Sav-a-Rama gave him $2.30 for the bottles. Wakefield was glad that the day hadn't been completely wasted as far as making money was concerned. He deposited the money in his cigar box, subtracted in his spiral notebook, and saw that he had $13.37 to go; $13.37 before everybody would be happy again. His mom called upstairs for him to set up the playroom tree. He guessed she was still trying to find things for him to do to keep him entertained.

That tree must have grown on the way home. Wakefield had to saw a foot off the trunk before it would clear the playroom ceiling. It certainly hadn't looked that tall in the woods.

He helped Sarah make decorations for it and even whipped up a few himself. They strung cranberries and popcorn, which they looped around the branches. They made birds from purple and pink foil, and created a new species of butterfly—gold, with red and green spots, and pipe cleaner antennae. They made Santas with cotton beards and fish with sequin scales and fruit sprinkled with silver glitter. Secretly, Wakefield thought the playroom tree looked better than the living room tree. But, of course, he didn't tell his parents this. They were proud of their tree, too.

He left Sarah to clean up the mess, because after all, he had to work on his ashtray, didn't he? His mom had brought it back from the ceramic shop, and he could hardly believe the change. It was bone white and very hard.

"Now for the glaze," Mrs. Quinn said. "Time's running out." She said that about a hundred times a day.

Wakefield chose a dark green, and his mom showed him how to stroke it on in thick globs. This had to be done three times, and it had to dry between each coat. The glaze didn't look green, it looked dull red.

"It will change color in the kiln," Mrs. Quinn assured him. "The extreme heat does it. You'll see. Now, let's take a look at the trees."

They examined each tree carefully. Then his mom said, "I think the living room tree deserves first prize." Wakefield looked disappointed. "But the playroom tree gets the grand prize." He cheered up again.

"I have an idea." Mrs. Quinn was smiling broadly. "Why don't you invite the Hennessey boy over to admire your tree? Perhaps you could become friends."

Mothers!

That night Wakefield heard himself being discussed

again. His mom said, "Wakefield seems to be his old self again. I think he had a happy day."

His dad yawned loudly and turned off the downstairs lights. "You see, Martha? I told you, you were making too much of the whole thing. The boy has no problems other than marking off the days until Christmas."

CHAPTER

8

On his way to breakfast the next morning, Wakefield remembered to give the Christmas trees some water. All the time he was filling the jar and carrying it over to the playroom, he kept remembering Mad Dog standing on the sidewalk simpering "Twismas twee." Mad Dog probably trimmed the Hennessey tree with poison arrows. In the doorway, he glanced up, blinked his eyes, and stopped short. Water sloshed out on the floor. Where was it? Where was the Christmas tree?

He pinched himself to make sure he wasn't sleepwalking. Ouch! He was awake all right, and the tree was gone.

He barreled across the hall and into the kitchen. His mom and dad were already eating breakfast.

"What did you do with the tree in the playroom?" Wakefield asked.

"Are you awake?" Mrs. Quinn was grinning.

"Sure I am. It's gone. There's no tree."

Wakefield's parents smiled at each other and, to humor him, got up and went down the hall toward the playroom. There were no glittering ornaments, no cranberry chains, no Christmas tree.

Mrs. Quinn turned to her husband. "Do you think Sarah could possibly have pulled it into her room?" Sarah adopted crazy things. For a whole month one time she slept with an oatmeal box named Tubby.

"I hardly think so," Mr. Quinn answered. "It's too big for her to manage." Wake and his dad knelt down to examine the empty space in the center of the playroom. Here and there they noticed a bit of colored paper or a stray cranberry.

"Look, Wakefield," his dad said, "These paper scraps and pieces of popcorn form a trail. They all lead to the back door." Just outside the door, a Santa Claus ornament lay on the wet sidewalk. His red cap had faded into the pink of his face and his white cotton beard.

"Somebody has stolen your Christmas tree," Mr. Quinn said. He and Wake stared at the streaky Santa, each wondering why.

"Martha," Mr. Quinn called up the stairs. "We've had a robbery. Better check the silver."

For the next ten minutes the whole family rushed around searching drawers and closets. Mr. Quinn was concerned about his tools and cameras, and Mrs. Quinn frantically looked in the out-of-the-way places where the Christmas shopping had been stashed. Wakefield checked his cigar box. They all met in the living room.

"Nothing has been taken but the children's tree," Mr. Quinn announced.

"Why just the tree?" Mrs. Quinn asked, but nobody was able to answer.

"We'd better call the police." Mr. Quinn went to the phone. "I don't like the idea of somebody's sneaking into our house while we're asleep. Who knows what our eccentric thief will fancy next?"

The conversation with the police sergeant did not go well.

"No, nothing of value, just the children's tree."

"No, there was no expensive lighting on it."

"Yes, we're sure it's not here. We've checked and double-checked."

"We've had a prowler about. At least, we think so."

"No, I don't know why anybody would want to steal a Christmas tree."

"A prank? I hardly think so."

When Mr. Quinn hung up, Wakefield was jumping up and down with excitement. He'd remembered something. "Mad Dog! It was Mad Dog! Call the police again!"

"Now, Wakefield, slow down." Mr. Quinn looked stern. "You can't accuse someone of stealing without proof. I know you don't like the Hennessey boy, but still—"

"Dad, he swore he'd get me. He was even teasing me about my Twismas twee."

"What would Mad Dog—don't any of your friends have proper names—what would he want with your Christmas tree?" Mrs. Quinn asked.

"That's just it," Wakefield insisted. "He does mean things for the fun of it; he never has reasons. Let's call the police."

"That's enough," Mr. Quinn said sharply. "We don't make slanderous statements in this house."

After that, things began to happen. The doorbell rang. A reporter from the *Courier* asked if he could get pictures and statements. He'd been sitting around the police station looking for a human interest story when the Quinns' call came in. Mrs. Quinn was trying to tidy the living room for the photographs, and Mr. Quinn was struggling to remember the children's ages for the captions underneath. Sarah came in, crying about her "boo-ful" lost tree, which delighted the reporter. He took fifty million pictures of her holding Foo Cat, tears running down her cheeks like Niagara Falls in the rainy season. They all trooped back to the playroom for more shots of Sarah pointing to the empty space where the tree had stood. Wakefield tried to slip away, but his mom pushed him in behind Sarah. All by himself he had to hold the ax which felled the tree while the shutter clicked again and again.

The whole thing was too embarrassing for words.

By lunch time the situation had calmed somewhat. At least, they'd stopped asking each other why? over and over. Wakefield stared at his sandwich and fidgeted. He had to get out of the house, and he'd better have permission. There was $13.37 to go and the days were racing by. He had the dark feeling lately that maybe he wouldn't get that $13.37. It was too terrible to think of. He could see Miss Booth, Imogene Cooke, his mom and dad, and the principal all looking at him. They were lined up like a firing squad.

"Mom,"—he'd decided that maybe the truth was the best way to go—"I'd like to make a little money." He hurried on before she asked why. "Could I try to get on

down at the shopping center selling Christmas trees?"

His mom and dad looked at each other.

"Martha, I think that would be all right. A boy needs a little spending money. Especially at Christmas."

His mom nodded agreement and gave him all sorts of instructions on where to call if he got bored, tired, sick, or whatever.

He left before they could have second thoughts.

Mr. Jensen at the Merry Yuletide Tree Center was glad to have the help. Jon, his regular assistant, was ill. "Boys come and go," he said. "Get a couple of bucks and take off. Are you good for all day?" he asked briskly. "That's six hours, you know."

Wakefield nodded. It didn't look like such a tough job; certainly nothing like shoveling snow. And it wasn't, he decided several hours later. But it was boring. Sometimes there'd be a whole hour with no customers—and then it was hectic. Four or five cars would drive up at the same time, each carload calling, "Boy! Over here, boy." He shifted from one foot to the other while the ladies decided that this tree wasn't bushy enough and that one had a hole in it toward the top. Nobody seemed to have the right change, and since he wasn't all that good in math, he had to be especially careful with his subtractions.

He and Mr. Jensen and Mr. Jensen's son warmed themselves occasionally at a fire in an old drum, but still he was never warm on all sides. His hands and face would burn, but his back, in between the shoulder blades, and his feet were always cold. Playing in the snow was not at all the same as working in the snow, he decided.

His gloves had two of the fingers out and the trees were sticky prickly.

Every now and then Mr. Jensen would say, "Still with us, Son? Not ready to give up, are you?"

Wakefield tried to smile each time.

His dad stopped by late in the afternoon and talked to Mr. Jensen. "Fine boy you have here," Mr. Jensen said, pointing to Wakefield. "Hasn't slowed down a bit."

Wake could tell his dad was proud.

"I think he's going to last out the day," Mr. Jensen said. "Most of them don't, you know."

Shortly before seven, Mr. Jensen switched off the string of lights that outlined the center, transferred his money from the cash register to a money bag, and doused the fire. He handed Wake an envelope with six one dollar bills in it, just as Mr. Quinn drove up.

"You've been good help, Son. The best I've had. Tell you what, why don't you pick out the finest Christmas tree in the lot? Take it home with you. Consider it a bonus."

"Oh no," Wake said. "Oh, no thanks, Mr. Jensen. Thanks anyway," he shouted, hurrying for the car. He never, ever wanted to see another Christmas tree as long as he lived.

CHAPTER

9

Sarah marked off the days until Christmas, and as each diagonal slash of red crayon appeared on the calendar, Wakefield's spirits sank lower and lower. Seven dollars and thirty-seven cents to go and not a single, solitary snowy walk in Highview. Mr. Jensen's assistant was back at work, and though Wake had looked along both sides of the sidewalk and down around the Burger Barn, there was not a soft drink empty to be found. At one time he'd thought he might find money on the sidewalk; now he couldn't even find a pop bottle. He'd asked a few places for work, but everybody said come back when you're sixteen. It was beginning to get more difficult to get away from the house. The Quinns' Christmas party was nearing, the situation was hectic, and more and more often he was being pressed into service. "Wakefield, do this, do that, do the other."

For several days Mrs. Quinn had been borrowing silver trays and cleaning and not allowing anybody near the living room. (That was okay by Wakefield. The room looked creepy, anyway, it was far too neat.) In the middle of everything his mom would put her head down on the table and say, "I just can't do it—fifty pepole." Then up she'd jump to make fancy arrangements with frosted pine cones and silvered magnolia leaves.

The day of the party she came back from the beauty shop with her hair all strange and swirly, still saying she couldn't do it. Wakefield couldn't understand grown-ups. Why have a party if it wasn't fun? She caught him staring at her. "Wakefield, you'll just have to help me. You'll have to stay up late, but one night won't hurt you."

"Sure, Mom." Staying up late beat going to bed any old day.

"Here's a Christmas card for you." She took a smudged envelope from her purse. "It came this morning, but I was so busy I forgot to give it to you." She hurried into the kitchen with a distracted look on her face. "Did I ever boil those eggs?"

It wasn't a Christmas card, but the note, signed "Mad Dog." The note read:

93

*I know where your Christmas
tree is — ha — ha — ha*

Wakefield wadded up the note as hard as he could and
threw it into the fireplace. To think that his dad dis-
approved of his "unreasonable attitude" toward Mad
Dog Hennessey!

On second thought, he needed that note. He pounced
on it just as the flames began to sear the edges. Now, he
thought, smoothing out the paper, his dad could have
his proof. There was no time for talking now, but after
the Few-Friends-In—

That night Wakefield showed the guests where to put
their coats and passed napkins and kept the nut bowls
filled. His mom was gay and happy and didn't once
complain about being tired. The ladies wore dresses of
gold and silver and deep red that rustled and sparkled
when they walked. They didn't kiss him or ask him to
recite or play the piano. The men asked him who was
going to win the Super Bowl game.

Everybody was talking about the stolen tree. The
Quinns had rated a full page on the front of the second
section, and all the guests had seen it. When the conversation shifted to price supports and the Middle East
situation, Wakefield lost interest, but he did enjoy the

carols. He was learning to sing harmony at school. At first he barely sang. Then he decided it sounded pretty good, so he sang louder and louder.

It was almost two o'clock in the morning when everybody left. Mrs. Quinn kicked off her shoes, and Mr. Quinn got out of his coat and tie in about two seconds. That was the latest Wakefield had ever been up in his whole life, but he drank a cup of spiced tea just to be sociable.

As he'd planned, Wakefield showed his parents the note from Mad Dog. They were not impressed.

"Anybody can read the newspaper," Mr. Quinn said, rumpling Wakefield's hair. "Drink up, playboy. It's already tomorrow."

The next morning Wakefield slept until eleven-thirty, the latest he'd ever slept. When he came downstairs, the family was eating lunch. His dad offered to fix him eggs and toast, but lunch looked better. Lunch was all the left-over fancies from the party.

His mom said, "Mr. Andrews called. He was at the party, you remember. He wants you to help out at the hospital this afternoon. His club is giving a Christmas party for the children who can't go home for the holidays."

This didn't sound like a paying job, but there weren't any paying jobs, anyway.

He went by the Andrews house—he couldn't think of a good reason not to—and was fitted up in a ridiculous-looking elf suit. Mr. Andrews looked pretty silly himself in a Santa Claus outfit, but Mr. Andrews said it was for the cause.

As Santa's helper, Wakefield's job was to pass out gifts to the children and help them untie. The little kids were happy and excited and screamed with laughter when Mr. Andrews went "ho-ho-ho!" All of a sudden Wakefield didn't think it was corny at all. He threw himself into the part and even used a squeaky elf-type voice, which made the little ones giggle. He had a good feeling about that outing, though he did feel sorry for the small boy in the big cast. Somehow, the boy reminded him of Tag-Along. He supposed it was the pale skin and the big sad eyes.

Strange. Tag hadn't been around in the last few days. Wake kind of missed him, sitting there on the steps blowing his bubble gum.

The day was not a complete loss, financially. Mr. Andrews' son, Ricky, had come to the party to play the guitar and sing. He asked Wakefield to help him with the evening paper route, since he was running late. The papers, the ones with the grocery ads, were almost as big as Sunday's—and it was dark before they finished. Most people were nice and said things like: "New man on the route, I see," or, "You look cold, want to come in and get warm?" But Mr. Gilbert Wood complained: "I expect my paper to be here at four-thirty. If you and Ricky want to fritter your time away hot-rodding and vandalizing, then don't take a job carrying the paper."

A little poodle nipped Wakefield on the ankle—all the time Mrs. Tichenor was saying, "Fifi won't bite. Fifi won't bite" And the bag strap broke—but mostly Wakefield enjoyed himself. He learned how to fold and tuck a paper—he'd always wanted to do that—and was two dollars and a half richer at the end of the route.

Wakefield did his accounts, subtracting in the spiral notebook and adding money to the cigar box, $4.87 to go. At one time he wouldn't have thought that was very much money. Now he knew how much work that represented, how little time there was left before Christmas, how few and scattered money-making operations were. Maybe Uncle Ernie's $5.00 would come in time. Maybe he'd have the $4.87 by December twenty-sixth. But it wasn't going to be easy.

CHAPTER
10

Uncle Ernie's Christmas card arrived on the morning of the twenty-fourth. Wakefield breathed a sigh of relief. His mother opened and read it aloud, but Wakefield was too excited to listen. Home free, he keep thinking. The five-dollar check, along with the money in the cigar box, would more than buy an aquarium. He'd have enough left over for a candy bar—a chocolate crispy or maybe a peanut buttter cup. Surely he deserved something for all his trouble.

His mother tucked the card back into the envelope.

Wakefield was confused. "Where's my check?" he asked.

His mother was confused, too. "Didn't you listen at all? Where's your mind, Wakefield? Uncle Ernie's coming here to visit, in January. Isn't that grand?"

Wakefield still didn't understand.

"I guess you didn't hear the very best part." She carefully tore the stamp from the envelope. "He's bringing you your Christmas present all the way from Germany. A cuckoo clock from the Black Forest."

"Oh, no," Wakefield groaned. "No money."

"Wakefield, I don't understand you. Your uncle goes to the trouble to choose and bring you a very special present, and all you can say is 'Oh no, where's my check?' You've become so mercenary. You acted exactly the same way about the fine quilt your grandmother sent. Where's your sense of values?"

Wakefield didn't answer. He traced designs in the rug with the toe of his shoe.

"I have some errands for you to do," his mother said in clipped tones. Wakefield was sorry to be the cause of his mother's disappointment. He wanted to tell her not to worry, that everything would be all right, but he wasn't sure things *would* be all right. There wasn't a way in the world, that he could think of, to raise the remaining $4.87.

He thought about it while he mailed letters, returned library books, and bought Christmas tree bulbs and small batteries, which was what his family always ran out of on Christmas morning. He'd made his purchases and

was waiting for the light to change when he saw him—
Mad Dog Hennessey—leaning up against the drugstore
window with that superior grin all over his face.

Wakefield simmered until the green flashed, then
charged across the street and marched right up to Mad
Dog Hennessey. He was too mad to think what he would
say, but the words spilled out anyway, fast and mean.
"Now listen to me, Mad Dog, I want that tree returned.
It's a rotten thing to steal a Christmas tree from a little
girl. Sarah's still crying about it. You see that our tree gets
back tonight. I don't care how or when, but that tree
comes back tonight. You understand?"

Wakefield took a step forward, and Mad Dog moved
back. "Sure, sure, if that's the way you want it," Hennessey said. He shook his head as though his mind couldn't
believe what his ears were hearing.

"I do indeed." Wakefield's eyes never left Mad Dog
or changed their expression. "I'm tired of your teasing
and dumb jokes, Mad Dog. You went too far this time."
Wakefield jabbed a finger at Hennessey's chest. "Get that
tree back. You hear? With everything on it—every last
thing."

"Yeah, sure Wake. I'll see that the tree gets back."
He stepped back and bumped into a sign post.

"Fine." Wakefield turned and walked away, leaving Mad Dog standing with his mouth open.

After he left Mad Dog, he walked aimlessly about town, not really knowing or caring where he was. In front of one of the department stores a little boy was crying and trying to get away from Santa Claus. The more his mother and Santa consoled him, the louder he howled. For a moment Wakefield wished he were two years old instead of almost ten. He'd like to fall on the sidewalk and kick and scream, too.

Imogene Cooke and her mother passed through the revolving doors then. Wakefield nodded, since Mrs. Cooke was there. Imogene lagged behind. "Don't forget our aquarium, Wakefield," she said. "Really, I don't know why Miss Booth didn't ask me to buy it. I certainly am trustworthy." She ran to catch up with her mother.

He walked back to the post office by the railroad tracks and counted freight cars for a while, wishing he could be on one click-clacking away from Imogene Cooke, away from his mother's hurt eyes, his father's stern ones, and the twenty-six pairs of shocked ones in Miss Booth's Four-B.

His eyes blurred from the names rushing by—Louisville & Nashville;—Southern Serves the South;—Canadian Pacific—and he looked away for a minute toward Tag's block. Catty-cornered across from Tag's, he caught sight of a large swinging sign. Lettered in block letters was word CASH. In smaller letters: *We buy and sell valuables.*

For the first time all morning, he knew exactly where he was going. Why hadn't he thought of it before? Tag had mentioned pawning things to get money for school supplies. He'd pawned the camera he won in a raffle and a transistor radio he'd gotten with popsicle wrappers. If Tag could do it, he could do it.

Uncle Jake's Pawnshop wasn't shiny like the department stores downtown. Nor was it decorated for Christmas. There were iron grill gates, pushed back now, with a padlock hanging from a chain on one side. The windows were grimy, and the dim showcases were crammed with banjos and guitars and dusty television sets. The sign in the window said *Instant Cash: Tools—Jewelry—Diamonds—Musical Instruments—Fishing Tackle—We Buy Old Gold.*

A man in a big, old-fashioned overcoat lounged outside, against one of the windows. His cheeks were red, his eyes a watery no-color blue, his whiskers were a black stubble outlining red lips. He watched Wakefield until Wakefield grew uncomfortable.

"You Tag's friend?" the man said.

Wakefield nodded.

"Thought so. You're on the wrong side of the tracks, ain't ya?"

Wakefield nodded and took off, walking very fast.

At home, he deposited his purchases on the hall table, and bounded up the stairs and into his room. The cardboard box from Sutcliff's was still under the bed. The outfit had long ago been put back into its original wrappings as best as Wake could arrange it. The flies were there, the top quality line, the single-action reel. Since the day he'd tangled with the curtain, the Geronimo 300 had never been used. He remembered how proudly he'd carried it home—and now he was looking for a chance to sneak it out! His mom and dad, however, and Sarah, too, seemed to be all over the house. Their voices came first from the kitchen and the back door, then the living room and the front door.

He recounted his money in the cigar box: $19.80. He checked all his figures, his subtractions by adding. *Was it possible that pawnshops closed early on Christmas Eve?*

"Your dad and I are going to make some deliveries," his mom called up the stairs. "The last two sculptures, and then I'll be free, free, free. Want to come along?"

"No, thanks." Wakefield tried to keep his voice offhand.

103

"We're taking Sarah and will probably celebrate by eating out. Sure you don't want to come along?"

"No, I think I'll just rest."

He heard his parents talking as they got their coats from the front closet. "Did you hear that, Martha? 'Rest,' he said. I really think we must take him to Dr. Giesel for a checkup."

Their voices waned to a murmur, the door slammed, and the house was quiet. Wakefield sat on the edge of his bed for five minutes in case his parents came back for some forgotten object. (He considered that five minutes the rest he'd told his mother he'd take.) Wasting no more time, he hefted the fishing rod over his shoulder and took off for Uncle Jake's Pawnshop. He was afraid to use the main streets—he didn't know where his mom had deliveries to make—so he skirted in and out, looking both ways at each intersection.

After he passed the post office, he slowed down a bit. He didn't think his mom had orders in this part of town. At least, she hadn't mentioned it. Then he thought of the closing time and sped up again.

The man was still there in front of the window. He was sitting on the sidewalk now, trying to light a cigarette between cupped hands. He looked up at Wake. "Got a match?"

Wake shook his head and gripped the rod.

"I'm Tag's dad," the man said.

"How do you do?" Wakefield answered politely and started to move on into the store.

The man called him back. "Does your daddy know you're pawning something?"

"No, sir," Wakefield said.

"Figures. Kids have no respect these days. Guess that thing belongs to your dad, don't it?"

"No, sir. I have to go now." Wakefield tried to smile, then darted into Uncle Jake's.

The man at the counter looked at him so long that Wakefield began to feel like a criminal. Finally the man —Jake—shifted his cigar to the other side of his mouth and looked down at Wakefield's package.

"Help you?"

"Yes, sir. I'd like to pawn this fishing rod and reel. It's brand new, never been used. A Geronimo 300."

"Is it hot?" the man interrupted.

Wakefield looked puzzled.

"I mean, did you steal it?"

"Oh, no sir." Wakefield's cheeks began to burn.

"I bought it myself with my own money." When he realized that he'd said with his *own money,* he became even more confused. "It's a rine fod. I mean a fine rod."

"Why you want to sell it then?" the man asked. He straightened the counter as he talked.

"I just have to, that's all." Wakefield mumbled.

"Speak up," Uncle Jake said. "Let's see it."

Wakefield put the package on the counter. The man grumbled because he had to untie and unwrap it. Wakefield tried to help him, but he was all thumbs.

Jake looked at the Geronimo 300, chewing on his cigar stub all the while. He tapped on the counter with his fingers and looked up toward the ceiling.

He said abruptly, "Five bucks."

"Five dollars?" Wakefield wasn't mumbling any more. He moved the rod closer to his side of the counter. "Five dollars? I paid $24.67 for that rod. It hasn't even been in the water. I only practiced with it one time and—"

"Take it or leave it," the man said, and turned toward the back room behind the shop.

"I'll take it," Wakefield said.

Without further comment, Jake rang up *No Sale,* and handed Wakefield a five-dollar bill and a cardboard slip with a number on it. He fastened another cardboard tag to the rod, and tossed it carelessly on the shelf behind the counter.

Mr. Toomey wasn't outside the store when Wakefield left, and Wakefield was very glad about it. Mr. Toomey

made him uneasy. No wonder Tag seemed mopey. Tag had to be around him all the time.

Wakefield had felt very depressed himself inside the store, but now he felt wonderful. For the first time in two weeks he felt glorious. He knew what his mother meant when she said she was free, free, free. He jumped up and grabbed at an icicle hanging from a lamp post. He scooped up a handful of snow and made a snowball and threw it at nothing, just to be throwing.

He threw back his head and shouted, "Yes, Imogene, O yes, I shall certainly buy your aquarium." He laughed all the way home, sliding on the ice, and wishing even complete strangers merry Christmas.

The pleasure he'd felt in buying the rod was nothing compared to the joy in getting rid of it. He thought about all the things he could do now. He wanted to look at Granny Quinn's quilt—before he couldn't bear to—but now he planned to go home and count every single little diamond. He was going to see what kind of design she made in the white part between the points of the star. She might have even embroidered in the date or his name. And his Uncle Ernie would be visiting soon with the genuine cuckoo clock, not one of your dime-store imitations, but the real thing.

He bounded up the steps and into the living room

humming "Jingle Bells." He even finished up with a little dance step and made an exaggerated bow before his mother.

Suddenly he realized that things were entirely too quiet.

CHAPTER

11

"Sit down," Mr. Quinn said.

Wakefield sat. He looked from one parent to the other. Their expressions were equally grim and unchanging.

"We want some straight answers," his dad said. "We were concerned about you, so we came straight home without stopping to eat. The phone was ringing when I opened the door."

Wakefield still didn't know what was the matter.

"It was Mr. Toomey," his mom said.

Wakefield knew then.

"Now, we know you went into Uncle Jake's Pawnshop," his dad said. "We know you were carrying a package. We want to know what it was, and why you went there. In short, we expect a strict accounting of what's been going on the last couple of weeks."

Wakefield cracked his knuckles and swallowed several times. He looked past his parents to the bronze figure sitting on the mantel.

Mrs. Quinn broke the silence. "We've made an effort to allow you more responsibility, now that you're older. Then you leave the house again today, without telling us where you are going. You didn't even bother to lock up. There are certain obligations that go along with privileges, you know."

Boy, did he ever know that! He'd had nothing but obligations since he'd bought that miserable Geronimo 300.

His parents were waiting—there was no escape. He took a final deep breath and plunged in, telling it from the very beginning: How grand the Geronimo 300 had looked in Sutcliff's window and how much he'd thought he needed it. He told about the lady who didn't pay him after he shoveled her walks, and about the dog that had bitten him on the paper route, and how he'd sat up late at night trying to untangle fishing line, and how he'd depended on that ten dollars from Granny Quinn and the five from Uncle Ernie.

He told his feelings, too. He explained how worried he was that he wasn't going to get the money back, and how terrified he'd be facing Imogene and Miss Booth and everybody if he didn't have that aquarium. He told his mom and dad how uncomfortable he felt when he couldn't tell them what was bothering him. It was miserable, he said, not having anybody to talk to.

Mrs. Quinn interrupted. "Didn't you think you could come to us with these problems?"

"Not exactly," Wakefield said. "I figured since I got myself into trouble, I'd have to get myself out. I did, too, but it sure wasn't easy."

"And you have now replaced all the money?" his dad asked.

Wakefield nodded. "I got the last five dollars at the pawnshop."

"That's good," his dad said. He was pacing the floor, his hands behind his back. He did the same thing when he was studying court cases.

They sat in silence for a few minutes. The clock ticked loudly. Then his dad came to a stop before the mantel, as though he were summing up before the jury. "As I see it," he said, "You've made restitution. That is, you've replaced the embezzled money."

"Embezzled?" Wakefield asked.

"Yes, you stole the funds entrusted to your care."

Wakefield hadn't thought of it that way, but since he

didn't have permission to use the money, he guessed "stole" was the right word.

"You also learned a valuable lesson about impulsive buying, which may come in handy later. Many adults make purchases that (1) they don't need; and (2) they can't use; and (3) they can't afford. In trying to pay for them—and you always have to pay, Wakefield—some people strangle themselves with interest charges. Others *can't* pay and get themselves into more serious trouble: lawsuits, bankruptcy proceedings, bad credit records."

Wakefield didn't exactly know what all his dad's words meant, but he got the general idea: *look before you leap*. That's what Aunt Glenna always said.

"You denied yourself some pleasures during Christmas vacation and worked very hard to collect that $24.67. In that, you showed perseverance, ingenuity, and responsibility."

The only word Wakefield recognized was "responsibility," which didn't sound so ugly anymore. He meant to look the others up.

"Yes," his mother said. "I'm very impressed with this new sense of responsibility."

Mr. Quinn smiled—finally—and thumped Wakefield on the back. "Yes sir, I think you're *almost* ready for a fly rod. You've grown up a lot lately. By this spring you

113

should be well able to manage a Geronimo." He hesitated, but only for a second. "That is, after you've saved enough money to reclaim it."

His mother was smiling and crying, too. Wakefield didn't quite know how she could do that, but she did every now and then. "Hey," she said, wiping her eyes, "I've been cheated out of my celebration. After I delivered Imogene Cooke, I was supposed to be wined and dined. Round up Sarah, Wake, and let's go. Name your restaurant."

"The Burger Barn?" Wakefield suggested.

His mother and father both groaned.

12

After they came back from the Burger Barn, Sarah hung up her stocking and left a snack on the hearth for Santa. She was still disappointed that there was no tree for the playroom, but Christmas Eve had come and Mad Dog hadn't. Wakefield watched at the window for him until he was forced to desert his post. His dad asked him to help assemble a cardboard supermarket which was giving him a rough time. Wakefield read directions while Mr. Quinn put "long screw E to side A."

"If the real supermarkets were this hard to build, we'd all starve to death," Mr. Quinn grumbled. Finally, the two of them got the play store together, all except one screw, which they never did find.

It was like old times, Wakefield thought. Now that he didn't have a guilty conscience, he could laugh and joke with his parents to a fare-thee-well. He didn't know what a fare-thee-well was exactly, but when Aunt Glenna was laughing to a fare-thee-well, she was laughing a lot, and he was enjoying his evening a lot. Everybody was in a good mood. He was cracking jokes, and his mom was chasing his dad with a sprig of mistletoe, and nobody mentioned fly rods and pawnshops.

The toy chest looked pretty with the colored lights of the Christmas tree shining on it. The play table was covered with a checked cloth Mrs. Quinn had made, and set with doll dishes. There were picture books, and games, and a panda bear propped in one of the chairs.

Mr. Quinn laid a fire ready to be lit the next morning, while Wakefield gathered up the cardboard cartons and wrappings and took them to the basement. His mom ran the sweeper and replaced burned-out bulbs on the tree.

"Let's have a cup of chocolate," she said, "and admire our work. It won't look like this long in the morning." The icicles on the tree shimmered in the lights, and the woodsy smell of pine filled the room. The toys were brightly colored and shiny with newness.

Wakefield thought his mom and dad were the best Santas in the whole world. He was glad he had taken the time to do a good job on their presents. Mom was right. The glaze on the ashtray came back from the kiln a rich, dark green. The planter looked as good as one from the store—even better, Dad said, because Wakefield had made it himself.

Mr. Quinn turned out the lights and went to the window to close the curtains for the night. Now he stood looking out, his hand still holding the cord. "Martha," he whispered, "come look at this." Mrs. Quinn and Wakefield both came.

There moving across the moonlit lawn came their Christmas tree. It seemed to be self-propelled, drawing closer and closer. The paper chains swayed back and forth. Occasionally the tree dipped a little, then righted itself and sailed on. As it inched out of view, the Quinns ran to the dining room to watch. In several minutes, it had turned that corner of the house and was approaching the back door. For a second or two, the tree paused, and there was a scraping sound.

"Somebody's getting our key we keep under the brick," Wakefield whispered. "Maybe now you'll believe what I say about Mad Dog."

All three held their breath while the door creaked open. Slowly the tree ducked under the door and stood upright in the back hall. When it began to lurch toward the playroom door, Mr. Quinn shot forward. Mrs. Quinn

117

switched on the light and everybody shouted at once.

There was rustling and writhing behind the tree. Branches swayed and ornaments shot off at all angles.

"All right, come on out of there," Mr. Quinn bellowed, dragging out something by the collar.

Wakefield just stood there, thinking about the look Mad Dog would have on his face. Even Mad Dog was no match for Mr. Quinn when he really got steamed up.

"What?" Wakefield and his parents all said at once. It was not Mad Dog who cringed before them. By no stretch of the imagination could this pale trembling creature be Mad Dog Hennessey.

"Tag?" Wakefield spoke softly. "Is that you?"

The boy nodded. He was too scared to speak.

"You stole our tree?" Wakefield asked.

Tag looked down at the floor and nodded. Wakefield noticed that he had on ripped sneakers and no socks. His nose was running, and he was crying softly.

"Come on into the living room, Tag," Mr. Quinn said. "You can tell us all about it."

"We'll have to get him warm first," Mrs. Quinn said. "Get a blanket, Wake, and see if there's any chocolate left."

Wakefield went away shaking his head. He simply couldn't believe it. Mad Dog, yes, but not ol' Tag.

When he came back again, Mrs. Quinn was speaking gently. "Now, calm down, Tag. We're not going to hurt you. We just want to understand why you took our tree." She tucked the blanket around him and handed him the chocolate. Tag was shaking so much the cup rattled against the saucer.

"I shouldn't have taken the tree. I know that. I was going to bring it back, though, even before Mad Dog told me I'd have to or he'd be in big trouble."

Oh boy, Wakefield thought. Mr. Big Mouth me had to accuse Mad Dog Hennessey. Oh boy! His dad had been right about proof positive.

"But why did you do it?" Mrs. Quinn insisted.

Tag's voice was smaller and smaller. "I watched you getting ready for Christmas. I looked in the basement windows and saw Wakefield making the————"

Everybody went "sh-h-h-h" at once. Wakefield remembered the different times he'd felt as if he were being watched. That was Tag.

"Anyway, everything looked like so much fun. I got to wishing more and more that I could be part of it. You know?" He looked up earnestly, trying to make them understand.

Mrs. Quinn nodded.

"I thought Wakefield's tree was the prettiest thing I

ever saw. When everybody went to bed, I took the key from under the brick—I've seen Wake get it there once or twice—and—I just took it, tree, stand, and all."

"I know that feeling," Wakefield said. "I really understand how you felt."

"Mad Dog knew I had the tree all along," Tag continued. "He peeps in the kitchen window when Pop's gone. Tries to scare me. He saw it the day after I brought it home." Tag took a deep breath. "Mad Dog said he

read in the paper that the FBI was after me. I thought he was probably teasing, but I was still afraid to come over here."

"That wasn't true, Tag. That Hennessey boy needs a ———." Mr. Quinn was sputtering. For once, he was being reasonable about Mad Dog, Wakefield thought.

Tag pretended that he wasn't crying. He cleared his throat several times, and Mrs. Quinn brought him more chocolate for his cough. "I haven't had a tree since Mom died. Let's see," he looked up to the ceiling and counted to himself, "that's four years now."

"All right," Mrs. Quinn said firmly. "The tree is back, the mystery is solved, and there's no harm done. Tag, you'll have to spend the night with us. It's too late to go home now. We'll let your father know you're staying."

"He ain't home," Tag said. "He took off again."

"Isn't," Mrs. Quinn corrected, just like Tag was one of the family. "We'll contact him later. Perhaps he'll let you spend the rest of the holidays here. Wakefield needs a boy his age to keep him company."

Mr. Quinn looked at the clock and whistled. "You boys had better get to bed. Tag, you can take the top bunk."

Later, Mrs. Quinn remembered to call up the stairway,

"Brush your teeth," but the boys had already shut the bedroom door.

"Hey, Wakefield. How'd you like that dance ol' Mad Dog did when I shot him with the beanshooter?"

"You were the one, Tag?" Wakefield's voice was hushed with wonder.

"Yep. Two times. I was up in the big pine tree by the post office. Ol' Mad Dog looked in garbage cans and every place, but he never once looked up."

They both giggled in the dark.

"You're all right, Tag. You really are," Wake said. Imagine that. Tag-Along Toomey getting the best of Mad Dog Hennessey. What a week this had been! Three late nights in a row. He yawned and told Tag goodnight. There were rustling noises downstairs. Santa? He yawned again, and the next thing he knew it was Christmas morning.

13

The rest of the family was already up. Wakefield slid under the bed and grabbed his mom and dad's presents. For the first time in his life, he hadn't thought too much about the presents *he* was going to get; he'd been so busy this vacation. Christmas was really going to be a surprise. He and Tag flew down the stairs and ran to the tree. Wake's gifts were stacked under a big poster-size card that said, "THANKS FOR THE HELP, WAKE-FIELD. Santa C."

"Neat-o!" he shouted. "Real tools!" They *were* neat. Not baby plastic hammers, but a real saw and wrenches and bags of nails and sandpaper. In the other packages were paint brushes and screwdrivers and a book—*A Hundred Projects for the Home Craftsman*. There were other presents, but Wakefield kept coming back to his tools for another look.

He gave his mom her present, and she was so happy she almost cried. Since it was Christmas, he let her give him a small kiss on the cheek.

Mr. Quinn said, "This beautiful ashtray goes right on my desk, and nobody is to touch it. I think it is magnificent. Did you truly make it yourself?"

Somehow there were also presents for Tag. (Hey, maybe there was a Santa! Or else sombody's parents were pretty clever.) There were detective books, a model airplane, a paint set, and a Yo-Yo. Tag pounced on the Yo-Yo and began to do all sorts of fantastic things with it. He did loop-the-loop and Eatin'-Spaghetti and Walkin'-the-Dog and Spank-the-Baby.

"Tag, you're really great with that. How about teaching me?" Wakefield asked. "Maybe we could have a show for some of the kids and charge." Mrs. Quinn objected to the word "charge," just as Wake knew she would—which is why he said it. It was a fun morning.

Mrs. Quinn caught the Yo-Yo in midair. "Tag," she said, "surely you must have another name."

"It's Theodore, Mrs. Quinn."

"That's a fine name, but a trifle long." She thought for a moment. "In this house I insist that you be called Ted."

125

Tag-Along, or rather Ted, beamed. Wake thought he might get used to calling Tag Ted, since it seemed to mean so much to Tag—that is, Ted.

His mom put carols on the record player. There was a special breakfast with lots of sweets. Ted was eating through the Danish pastries as though he might not ever get another whack at them. The living room was comfortably messy again, and the fire crackled and hissed. Wakefield and his dad were singing "The Twelve Days of Christmas" and having a good-natured argument over whether it was ten drummers drumming or ten lords a' leaping.

Sarah was having a fine time, too. But just wait until she gets to be nine, Wakefield thought. When she was old enough to put a little more into Christmas, she could get a lot more out of it. He smashed a nut on the hearth with a flatiron—nobody could ever find the nutcrackers on Christmas morning—and announced to the whole family: "Nine—just before ten—is the very best time to have Christmas."

Ted agreed.

June Lewis Shore

With a family that includes her husband, Ken, four daughters, a son, and Samson, the St. Bernard, the Christmas season is very real to June Lewis Shore.

"We enjoy traveling," she says of them. "The Canadian Rockies and Vancouver Island last year; Maine and Nova Scotia this year—and between major vacations, shorter treks (in a red school bus) for fishing or camping. We often attend craft and folk music festivals in Appalachia. (As an only child, I occasionally find so much togetherness overwhelming, and I retreat to my books and painting.)"

Although they have lived in Michigan and British Columbia, home for the Shores is Jeffersontown, Kentucky, near Louisville.

Holding a bachelors degree with a major in English and art, June Shore has taught both subjects as well as special education. A writer, too, she has published fiction and nonfiction magazine pieces. *What's the Matter with Wakefield?* is her first book.